THE **KEEPER'S** DAUGHTER

Also by Jean-François Caron

Novels
Nos échoueries

Poetry
Des champs de mandragores
Vers-hurlements et barreaux de lit

The Keeper's Daughter *is the*
first novel to be published in English.

THE
KEEPER'S
DAUGHTER

JEAN-FRANÇOIS CARON

Translated by W. Donald Wilson

Talonbooks

Talonbooks
278 East First Avenue, Vancouver, British Columbia, Canada v5T 1A6
www.talonbooks.com

First printing: 2015

Typeset in Arno
Printed and bound in Canada on 100% post-consumer recycled paper

Interior and cover design by Typesmith
Cover photograph © Ömer Ünlü via Flickr (CC 2.0) http://www.kolayfotograf.net
Back cover photograph © Giannis Angelakis via Flickr (CC 2.0)

Talonbooks gratefully acknowledges the financial support of the Canada Council for the Arts, the Government of Canada through the Canada Book Fund, and the Province of British Columbia through the British Columbia Arts Council and the Book Publishing Tax Credit.

This work was originally published in French as *Rose Brouillard, le film* by Éditions La Peuplade, Saguenay, Quebec, in 2012. We acknowledge the financial support of the Government of Canada, through the National Translation Program, for our translation activities.

Library and Archives Canada Cataloguing in Publication

Caron, Jean-François, 1978–
[Rose Brouillard, le film. English]
    The keeper's daughter : Rose and the archipelago of shifting memories / Jean-François Caron ; translated by W. Donald Wilson.

Translation of: Rose Brouillard, le film.
Issued in print and electronic formats.
ISBN 978-0-88922-920-4 (PBK.).—ISBN 978-0-88922-921-1 (EPUB)

    I. Wilson, W. Donald, 1938–, translator II. Title. III. Title: Rose Brouillard, le film. English.

PS8605.A7595R6713 2015   C843.6   C2015-901196-5
                                            C2015-901197-3

*Countries are born in memory, and
memory doesn't lack imagination.*

— PIERRE PERREAULT

THE

KEEPER'S

DAUGHTER

I'll be all, everybody. I'll be the lot:
their voices, I'll take on all of them.

I'm an archipelago.

First, I'm Dorothée who wants to feed the starving, as she looks at the screen showing what she was able to film. And then there's Vigneault the sacristan, just before the ferry.

The old woman was alone. The story couldn't begin any other way. That's how it will end.

Perched on a tripod in a corner of the kitchen, my camera points at her. A close-up of her face. Her stoic eyes. Her pores, ocean deep, glistening from all the tears they've had to absorb. Her broad nose filling the whole space. A few strands of too-fine hair. Neither really long, nor really short. Her uncared-for hair (the hair of an uncared-for old woman), its state betraying its former tendency to curl gently, and betraying also its neglect by a forgetful old woman. A forgotten old woman.

I use the first few minutes of the taping to explain to her who I am, where I'm from, and why I've come. She doesn't hear. As soon as she sees me, she calls me Dorothée. Dorothée, the African girl. She repeats it. To make sure I understand. Dorothée, the African girl. It's no use telling her I was born in Port-au-Prince, or that since I turned two the sky of Quebec is the only one I've laid eyes on, or that Dorothée is not my name at all: she doesn't hear anything.

Rose Brouillard hears only herself. That's not so bad. Okay then, I'll be Dorothée.

The interview took place in Rose's apartment. To the relentless tick-tock of the clock on the kitchen wall. This was the moment I'd been waiting for. That I'd been planning for so long. That I'd turned this way and that, long before. And it was over too soon.

Bringing it off was a major victory. They'd warned me in the office at Plumules Nord. It was Jérôme, the guy with the beard and the crook-toothed smile, when he asked me straight out: Do you know what would be great? It would be to find the Keeper's daughter and get her to tell about how she used to live back then, shut away on that island. She'll probably have lots to tell, you know how it is with old folk and their yarns. You could even bring her back onto the island. Just think if she agreed: taking her back on the island and having photos taken of her to show the tourists that'll come! Think human interest! The tourists will just love that, to see that thanks to us, she's come back to where she was a child, how she shed a few tears when she went back into her restored home – she's sure to cry – and how she laughed remembering the way she used to play along the shore. They'll love seeing her in the photos and recognizing her in the very spot they're visiting! They'll feel close to her. Of course it won't be easy, he said, it won't be easy at all. He admitted that he'd already done some asking round the village at the start of the project, and that no one knew where she was. That's what you were hired for, you know.

That's what I was hired for.

In the village, like you'd expect, half the people didn't have a clue who I was talking about. Rose Brouillard didn't mean a thing to them, not even the oldest ones. Some of them knew nothing about the Keeper, not even that his island existed. Really odd.

Jérôme, who looks after the paperwork for all the company's developments, had warned me. But I never thought it would take me so long to find Rose Brouillard. Her life was so loose-knit. When I finally thought I'd gotten a hold of it my fingers would slip through – through the gaps between the stitches, through the spaces, getting entangled, pulling stitches: here a knit, there a purl . . .

I'd have to comb through all of Onile's notebooks and track down the few rare characters in his story, in flesh and blood. The ones still alive were even rarer. For the two rows of graves in the little cemetery of Sainte-Marée-de-l'Incantation, on the height behind the village, have nothing more to tell. Just the silence that comes through the railings. Or maybe a murmur, it too buried by the wind.

So, find the ones who've survived and retained a few flimsy memories of them. Go from one to another, introduce myself, ask questions, listen to their confessions, unravel what they have to tell of the story of the Keeper and his Brouillard daughter.

Understand. Question. Jot down a few relevant anecdotes to pad out my file. But mostly leave empty-handed, surprised at the bafflement of some when I mention the Brouillards and their island. The people of Sainte-Marée, the ones I questioned, lose themselves in the remembrance of their own past. I'd have a long way to go. A long way and a long time.

Until at last I found this old guy, this Monsieur Vigneault. Once the village sacristan, now a widower and bent on remaining one, he's preferred to hold his tongue all his life, listening instead to what others had to say. Being a sacristan you give the impression you're close to God. So it's to the sacristan that people turn when they need absolution but dare not go directly to the priest. He's heard a lot of stories that way.

He's never gone in for storytelling himself, Vigneault the sacristan, or so he says. That didn't stop him from being very generous and obliging once I'd found him. As well as his weird jokes (three times he told me with equal relish about the swan that went crazy because it broke out in goosebumps), he strung me off a few pearls of no great significance, old yarns the villagers used to tell over and over, in the days when he was still among them. Stories I added to my stock.

Now that priests have become missionaries again, now that there are so few of them that they wear themselves out visiting the faithful all over the district, Monsieur Vigneault the sacristan has retired and sought refuge in the city. Until he goes to church again between the mahogany boards he's chosen from the Caron & Fils catalogue, his heart will beat at La Pointe, not far from the falls, on the little rue Racine. The one in the middle of nowhere. The dead end you have to look forward to at his age.

While he was dishing me up a few generalities about Onile and his daughter, his hands danced and scrabbled in his unkempt hair, struggling to come together in front of his mouth when he coughed. He coughs a lot, the old sacristan. He sputters long, twisting gobs.

3

It's on account of the incense at Mass, or the priests' pipe tobacco. Once you know, you back off.

Back on the dock: Vigneault the sacristan is coming up behind me, but I don't see him, I've no idea he's there. I can feel discouragement taking me by the throat, unsettling me, all of a sudden knocking me off balance. All my efforts will amount to nothing if I can't flush out more than the old stories I've already been told. The company needs more than that for its project. The tourists have to be fed, for they have the tourists' hunger: curiosity. As for me, I want even more than that: I want to feed History. Gluttonous History. History that is never done consuming.

Here I am, standing on the dock, waiting to board the ferry, with my hand luggage, my camera case, the lot. The humidity is frizzing my hair, though it's straightened and slicked down at the sides. In the grip of the unusually powerful onshore wind, I never heard Vigneault the sacristan calling my name. When the wind blows like that, it's what you hear. Nothing else.

I'd like to have a presence like that, like the wind's. Enveloped in my flapping windbreaker, I'm trying to learn.

Monsieur Vigneault took me by surprise, coming up from behind with a gleam in his eye and a tight-lipped smile, barely able to breathe through his nose because of the blast trying to fill it, to scour his bronchial tubes. He started coughing again before he could get a word out. His gnarled old hand just gripped mine and pried, trying to force it open. He wanted to stuff a torn, crumpled scrap of paper into my palm. Scratched in the shaky hand of an old man who all his life has hardly ever had to write anything except for the same old church words over and over. I was able to read: *Rose Brouyar*. With an address on rue Drolet in Montreal – spelled *Drolette*.

I'm Vigneault the sacristan in his empty apartment on little rue Racine in the middle of nowhere. Dorothée's absence-perfume still hangs in the air.

It's empty, my apartment. Like before she came, the little black girl. Though she nearly stayed: I kept on chatting, chatting to her even after she was gone. That's how it is when someone pays me a visit: there's too much to say clogged athwart my heart, so once they're here, once I get started, there's no holding back. I talked to her. To her, with her standing back. Addressed her person in the half-open door. Addressed the closed door. Addressed the empty air, where something like her perfume still lingered, listening for her. So I went on telling: Rose Brouyar, in the fragrant absence of a young-black-woman-now-departed-the-scene. Spouted the same stories, but fuller, better, bigger. Like that, she'd have believed them. I'd have convinced her.

I told on till it choked me, the way it does. Talking till then, till the spittle went down the wrong way – almost none, it takes very little, but then there's that crude, rending cough, that sapping cough that leaves you no chance of going on, gagging and strangling me every time I get going. Then, instead of unburdening myself to the silence of her now entirely absent person, I thought:

Rose Brouyar,
Rose Brouyar,
The Keeper's Rose.
Rose Brouyar.

And I thought on: for sure someone must know – does know, knows where she is, if she's not dead, may she rest in peace, someone must know.

I'm Vigneault the sacristan in his empty apartment on the little rue Racine, about to see a vision.

Like a holy image: my cousins, the three flowers, appearing, as true as I'm standing here, in the void of my apartment, in the silence of that fresh absence, the three sisters standing there, beatific plaster saints, smirking and smiling with their oohing and aahing and Call us (I think). On their lips I could read as clear as day, in a floral chorus: Call us, come and see us. Now there's a good idea, so it is! Yes, my cousins, they knew about Rose Brouyar, for sure. They knew, yes, they did.

So I called.

5

**Now I'm Fleur, or Flore, or Florence. Beside her, her
two sisters, a floral chorus under a leafy canopy,
somewhere between Montreal and Sainte-Marée.**

We are Fleur, Jacinthe, and Marguerite. I'm Fleur, the youngest,
my name's Florence, but never mind, they *call* me Fleur, and often
Flore. I'm the littlest one, always on her feet, the energetic one, the
one who welcomes guests, offers a cup of coffee, a plate of shortbread,
the one who has all her teeth, so usually the one with the broadest
smile, a totally uninhibited smile, a big wide one. I'm a young old
maid of sixty-eight – or just an old maid, it depends. I wear the same
pleasant expression all day long – at least I try, just in case someone
should come.

It's me, Fleur, who does the gardening, the weeding, and the
yardwork, sniffing the breeze off the river. It's me hears the sightseers
going by on the other side of the thick hedge, the things they tell one
another, the things they don't. Of course I don't enjoy it as much
since the village has been invaded by tourists.

Sainte-Euphrasie, now there's scenery for you, yes sir, with
one of the most beautiful sunsets in the world, at least according
to *National Geographic*. Anyway, it's our pride and joy in Sainte-
Euphrasie, and even though no one can turn up a copy of the
magazine that testified to it, no one doubts it, no one asks themselves if there might not be one just as beautiful somewhere else,
maybe at Saint-Pierre-du-Portage, La Bouteillerie, or La Pointe.
You just have to see it, it's there every evening, you can't miss it:
beauty and colour spread over the murky North Shore, splashed
on the river's iridescent surface, veining it like a slab of Cuban
marble. It's enough to bring floods of tourists.

But tourists, we know what they are. Or, rather, we don't know
who they are. They're not like the village folk, you don't know them,
you don't know where they're from, who they take after, who they're
descended from, so their scraps of stories are mostly of no interest.
Anyway, once they're past the hedge all they talk about is me, the
youthful old woman bent over her petunias or her rose bushes, for
it's so quaint to see me stooping like that in front of my pretty little

house with its weather-beaten cedar shingles, enclosed by the slender frame of an almost-view over the river. Byootifool. Reely byootifool. Reely byootifool, they say, or something like that, that's what it sounds like when I say it, that's the way my sisters hear it. Byootifool. Reely byootifool. Byootifool. Reely byootifool.

Some of them even give me a wave, me, the little old woman bent over her rose bushes, so I put on my pleasant smile, raise an arm, pruning shears in one hand, blink prettily in a ray of sunlight to make it look picturesque, then readjust my hat to make it picture perfect, and I bend over my roses or petunias again, cutting them, or pretending to. I can't remember all they say, but I count the ones who wave. Then I tell my sisters where they were from and how they spoke: Hai, auw are you? Byootifool gardenne, reely byootifool. That's what they say.

I'm Flore, still. And now, her sisters, so that we know who they are.

My sisters: Jacinthe and Marguerite, they come as one package, you have to talk about both at the same time, in the same tone of voice, like a tidbit you have to take in a single bite. When you say Jacinthe and Marguerite they're not separate, they're linked by the *and*: two coordinated women. That's the way they're joined: Siamese twins in their speech and their habits, one in all but the flesh, so that people would always combine them in the same sentence, or speak to one or the other, never differentiating, expecting one to answer for the other and vice versa.

Actually, they're not really Siamese twins, Jacinthe and Marguerite, but they are twins – eighty-two-year-old twins who have always lived as one, always or almost always sleeping in the same room, always or almost always wearing the same clothes, playing with the same pack of cards, taking turns to read the same books – though now and again reading aloud together, to bring them more alive, watching the same movies and telling the same stories, taking turns to add their two cents' worth.

Despite that, there's no confusing them, Jacinthe and Marguerite. The Jacinthe of the two is the one with curly hair. But she's also the one with a life, the one who smokes, whose teeth are stained brown, the one with the throaty voice, the reliable one, the one who travels and sometimes still goes on dates, the one who can always find someone despite her smoking and her brown teeth, for she's lively and a good dancer. She very nearly ended up in Port-Cartier with a bald young seventy-five-year-old. That was two years ago. But no, putting a river between herself and her sister (not me – that's not the same thing – but her Marguerite), that was too high a price to pay for picking up some poor devil who was mostly looking for someone to feed and groom him. A man-dog, that's what Jacinthe likes to call him. Tame enough, but needing a lot of care. And she laughs every time she says it, with the same hoot. A man-dog. Jacinthe's laugh. A man-dog. Another hoot.

You'd suspect she had some regrets about the whole affair. She returned home without a word, not a single word, with her heart patched up as best she could, and resumed life with her two sisters, Marguerite and me, smoking outside, watching me garden, playing cards with Marguerite on her good days, and tolerating her on her bad ones. For Marguerite, the Marguerite of the pair, does have her bad days.

Marguerite is the elder twin (and the eldest of us three). And those extra three minutes of life, before her fellow emerged in turn from between her mother's thighs, seem to have cost her dear.

For Marguerite is the messed-up one, the worn-out, broken one of us, with her body bent double as if her back has failed her. So she has her stick, her braces, and her corset, but even then she sometimes gives up walking and just sits on the porch. We help her there, arm in arm, and she stays sitting there with her head leaned backwards, staring into the leafy canopy, attempting to catch a glimpse of grey or of river-sparkle ignited by the breeze, in the green purgatory of her silent suffering. Sometimes she can't walk, can't keep upright, can't keep any way.

Multiple sclerosis. One woman in a thousand. One woman in a thousand, and it had to be her. Not her twin, nor me, her other sister. Just her. She's the broken one of us three, the most broken of all.

I'm Dorothée entrapped by seasickness, taking stock, with no piece of paper in her hand. We'll also mention the three sisters' stratagems, including the seventy-six card trick.

The river is tossing us about, it'll be a long crossing. It's not that I'm very prone to seasickness, but when the horizon plays peekaboo through the portholes in the main passenger lounge as they swing violently, oscillating between the open water and the pale sky, then I have to admit I soon feel nauseous. When we're rolling so hard I go out on deck, taste the salt spray on my lips, and greet the wind. Together, they almost settle my stomach. Probably it also helps to keep my eyes fixed on some spot on shore, always the same – not where the opposite dock is, but where the archipelago is, off to the east.

Just after my visit Vigneault the sacristan called a cousin of his. She's an old maid who lives with her two sisters, as old as herself and as spinsterish, some distance away in the stifling verdure of Sainte-Euphrasie, a village along the shore. The three of them make a fine lot of true gossips, according to Monsieur Vigneault. It seems their almost encyclopaedic information about everyone's comings and goings has a track record.

Under the leafy canopy of the compact little village, squeezed in where the river and the cliff meet, an old cedar-shingled house. It's the headquarters of an incessant data-gathering enterprise. Since they had nothing to do but be at odds all day, the sacristan's three cousins decided to relieve the boredom by collecting information about everyone and their dog. They used several ploys, but one was especially effective: each year they sent out simple greeting cards – a winter landscape, a Christmas tree, or beribboned packages adorned with gilded or coloured balls. Each contained a few lines of commercial verse, and was signed by all three. Just before Christmas the cards reach everyone listed in their impressive address book, a leather-bound volume with nature-inspired ornaments on the cover that Jacinthe had bought from a craftsperson – it was on one of those rare trips she'd taken with her man-dog (Jacinthe's laugh). Into this book, which contains the meticulously copied names and addresses of all their acquaintances, the ones still living but the dead as well, are also inserted a few disparate pages, required by the corrections arising from the peregrinations of their many contacts.

Seventy-six cards last year, signed, sealed, stamped, and addressed in the hand of one or other of the three sisters – usually Flore or Jacinthe. In the immaculate script of well-educated ladies.

Seventy-six cards last year. Seven fewer than the year before. There's no point sending cards to the ones who've passed on.

Seven fewer than the year before. That had been a big year.

Seventy-six cards last year. A nice gesture. But above all a clever stratagem, signing and mailing greeting cards in order to catch echoes of others' lives. For most of those who receive them feel obliged to answer, and strew their conventional missives with clues that the three old maids apply themselves to deciphering. And if perchance a card is returned, they learn that so-and-so has died or moved (you can never be sure which), bringing fresh grist to their latest tittle-tattle.

It was Monsieur Vigneault the sacristan who explained all this, in his man-who-rarely-speaks voice, strangled by a dry cough.

Who can tell what yarn he had to spin to wangle the information out of them? His cousins must have regaled themselves for several days on that strange tale. They tried to get more out of him, but Vigneault had managed to get the address. Rose Brouillard's address. And that was well worth a few scraps of trivial gossip.

It didn't matter that the wind and the open sea had snatched away the piece of paper a few minutes after Vigneault the sacristan left. The river guards its stories jealously, but I'm making progress. Now I know there's a good chance that Rose Brouillard is still alive. And that I'll find her on rue Drolet, in Montreal. I just have to search, it's a matter of days. Long enough to track her down. To meet her.

Never mind the raging river, this wind is doing me good. The island landscapes have a salty taste. Before long, I'll be with Rose.

I'm Fleur, or Flore, or Florence, discussing men
in love, the sort she's familiar with.

I get about three of them every ye~
people too much in love, or whose lo~
my sisters: I had a lover today. That~
the thought of me having a lover ~

.The lovers notice the roses, an~
them, they pluck up courage to come acros~
sometimes full of dollars, and ask for my roses: ~
madam, totally shameless, but perhaps, just perhaps ~
the favour, the great, the enormous favour, of allowing me ~
a few of your roses; it's for the one I love, the one I hold so dear.
And they all have the same harassed look, you can never tell if it's
because of love or some crisis, or if it's because they think at last
they've found what they're looking for – anything would have done,
but this old lady's roses, my roses, they're something else all the
same, the roses from this old lady named Fleur, it's extraordinary,
a thing she's sure to remember for the rest of her life, this birthday,
these roses bought from an old lady named Fleur.

So, with the lover looking on, I choose the best, cut them with
a long stem, strip the leaves from the angled end, slice off the
thorns for them to be held, and finally pluck off any flawed petals,
for the gift of a rose must be perfect. Next, a bed of greenery to lay
them on: a few fern leaves from the patch under the big maple will
be just the thing. I choose the freshest ones, and a nice sparkle
comes into the lover's eyes, for he's imagining himself presenting
them, but above all because he can be sure he hasn't committed
a faux-pas this time, that no one else would have thought of this,
of giving these very special flowers, the flowers from the old lady
named Fleur.

That makes my sisters laugh.

I'm Dorothée (before being renamed Dorothée). She's in an apartment
you have to get out of because it's too hot, and it's absolutely not
there that the story takes place. And then there's the death of
Billie Holiday, the blues singer, the one they called Lady Day.

11

ut for three days in the big city. So, toss a suitcase on the
ambitious suitcase, wide open, jaws gaping on the bed as
ur the room and me with it. Leave this voracious suitcase on
, then rifle the closet to feed it: the first three blouses, white,
, and strawberry, the first three pairs of shorts, some culottes,
atever, and the underwear, the stockings, add a sweater that'll
probably be useless, put it all in a pile, chuck it almost violently into
the yawning maw of the suitcase that's growing impatient on the bed,
almost flinging them, but not in anger, not at all, just for the pleasure of
doing it quickly, without any care or attention, for the suitcase is too big
anyway and none of it matters. Then zip up the gaping jaws and collect
brushes – toothbrushes, hairbrushes – from the bathroom counter as
I go by. A streak of pee in the bowl, don't forget the camera case, all
packed for the trip, then shut the apartment door on the sweltering
heat before the toilet has ended its boisterous gargle. I knew perfectly
well it was a bad idea to rent on the third floor in a neighbourhood of
asphalt, car parks, streets, and concrete curbs, tucked in behind the
shopping centres, the gas station, and the bowling alley. I thought I'd
be away from home a lot, but not that I'd want to get away so badly.
So, shut the door on it, on the concentrated, accumulated heat, shut
the apartment door on it.

I hate the highway. It never sings, never talks, never satisfies,
never dazzles. It's a soporific, a lethal dose you have to reject. And
I reject it. I opt for the long way.

Now there are just five hours' driving with windows down,
or maybe six, depending on the route I choose, with the wind on
my neck – an interminable stint. Until I reach the air-conditioned
hotel room where he arranged to meet me. In the city. The big city.

Between here and there the road improvises a cluttered display. It's
still early July, Quebeckers have just been moving house, so you find
all kinds of stuff on the road: a spoon on the median strip of an urban
avenue, frayed balls of blue wool in the middle of the street as if tangled
in the yellow dotted lines on the roadway, a battered drinking fountain
standing on a riverbank like some conceptual environmentalist ad,
soiled furniture on the sidewalks of villages divided by the road and
in neighbourhoods of towns you traverse at full tilt.

Inside the car, Billie Holiday rasps at my heart from some old pirated recordings that I've been playing endlessly for weeks, a polluted music in which you can hear the needle scratching on the vinyl with a light, repetitive crackle. Keeping all four car windows open is no longer enough to allow in the breeze I want to feel on my body. It's hot.

The sun visor on the driver's side simply fell off two summers ago. It crumbled away as if it had been baked. My face is bathed in sunlight. Inside my head, bright spotlights fleck Lady Day's face and spatter a black grand piano that disappears, so powerful is the singer's presence. A wind off the river.

I'm Lady Day near the black piano that reflects the spotlights and on which she has just set down her empty glass.

It's so hot here, under the lights. I'm sweating in the coils of blue smoke: my forehead, my temples, my underlip are flecked with droplets of perspiration. Someone offers me a handkerchief, I wipe my forehead and the back of my neck, never faltering, never slowing, nor dying. I'm not dead. My name is Billie Holiday, and I'll never die.

I'm Dorothée in the heat of her car. There's the wind, not enough of which is getting in, and there's Lady Day singing even louder.

She's not dead, Billie. She'll never die. I feel cooler when I think of her. Or maybe a cloud drifted across the sun. I'm clouded over, as they say. It's likely just that, a cloud. The asphalt turned darker when the sun ended its onslaught; I'm not the only one not burning so hot. I slow down to enjoy this spell of greyer light.

The display on my Pontiac's dash shows it's thirty-two degrees outside. It's really the only gadget on this old car that still works. That, and the power windows, fortunately. It was fully loaded once. That was before I bought it, just when it was starting to fall apart. After 327,000 kilometres, the extra features are worn out. But she's not a goner yet, this old Pontiac. She should last till Montreal. If not, I'll abandon her. I don't care.

Lady Day is dead. It was her liver, pickled in alcohol. It was her kidneys, poisoned by alcohol. It was fatigue, aggravated by alcohol.

Whatever the biographies say, she must have been magnificent, even in death. When they wiped the sweat from her forehead, temples, lips, and neck. Resolutely facing her last spotlight. July 17, 1959. It was hot. Just like today.

Fifty-two years later, it's hot, even with Highway 132 going by at a hundred an hour, and Billie isn't dead anymore, never will be again. She's filling my ears, turned up full blast, to bury the wind. Lady Day will bury the wind.

Rose isn't dead either.

I hope Rose isn't dead. I hope she'll wipe her brow. I can do that for her. I hope she'll sing, maybe. That she'll sing. For my camera.

Before I go to the hotel I think I'll give it a try. Pay her a visit right away, go to her place. Film the neighbourhood. Rue Drolet. All Villeray. Saint-Denis. And I'll knock on her door.

I'll knock on her door.

I'm Dorothée sitting in her car that she's pulled over beside the 132, in an unfamiliar village. In her head there's a wall of old men, one grumbling louder than the rest.

In one of the villages dotted along the 132, freeze-frame. I open a bottle I filled with water before leaving home. It's lukewarm. More than lukewarm: warm. It doesn't quench my thirst at all.

The houses here all sit along the roadside, crammed together. Piled together like that, they evoke pleasing images.

They remind me of the stacked stones of Sainte-Marée's little walls. Clinging to the hillside as it did, the village forced the first inhabitants to construct stone terraces on which to build their houses. Seen from the river, even the highest of them seem to stand at the water's edge, heaped one on top of the other. Directly below the fields that open up across the plateau.

They remind me of those stones. I've got pictures of them in my archive.

They remind me too of the old village men bunched together on the quay, fishing for capelin. They're a wall of old grousers, with two or three younger ones wedged in between. Plus the few tourists that sometimes try their hand. A wall of old grousers, a rampart that keeps the kids away from the edge. They mill about in the rear, a boisterous, excited pack.

They remind me of those old guys fishing. I should go and film them and slip in a few sequences during the editing.

I'm Dorothée with her camera, filming the old men fishing on Sainte-Marée quay.

Go play somewhere else!

That's the oldest one, the blind one – not completely blind but just enough to boast, or complain, about it. He's the oldest, puffing away on a hand-rolled cigarette stuck in his mouth beneath a yellow-stained moustache. He doesn't fish anymore, this old blind one, his fishing days are done, he just sits at one end of the line of old guys wedged on the dock, and asks: So, are they biting? So, are they coming? A couple of dozen, I don't call that biting. It's the whales, that's what it is, they can't hunt them off anymore, it's the whales that eat all the fish. Then it's the ships, fouling up the river with the poisons they bring from far away. They empty barrelfuls of dead stuff off the decks into the river water just opposite, they say.

He doesn't fish anymore, the old blind guy. He doesn't fish anymore, but he's there, he's an expert. You've got to rip out their eyes with the hooks, he says, pointing at them. Can't stomach that, young fella? You have to fish with the eyes, or you'll get nothing but your two dozen, that's for sure. Young folks today, they don't know how to fish for their supper. I reared my children on capelin, so I did, and I used the eyes for bait. Yes sir! Unless you use the eyes you never catch anything. No siree!

His fishing days are done, the old blind guy at the end of the line of old guys on the dock, yet he's there: Go play somewhere else! That's what he's always shouting at the kids that are saved from falling in by the tight wall of old guys. Then the kids go down on the beach on the other side, where they hold the incantation on Fridays. They throw pebbles into the choppy water that stirs the seaweed and the thick mosses. Then the old guys are left in peace, and the old blind one rolls himself another smoke, with the wind blowing a few shreds of strong-smelling tobacco off the dock into the murky water that slaps against the stone of the jetty. The same stone that was used to build up the village, terrace upon terrace.

I'm Dorothée sitting in her car. She has parked it in this unfamiliar village with the 132 running through it.

Let's get things sorted out: back to the little village by the 132, the unfamiliar one. I wonder if there's one house older than the others. An old blocked-up house, taking up space in the village. There's a handful of children squabbling on the sidewalk, near a French-fry stand that reeks of cooking oil. They're quarrelling over a haul of empty bottles to be returned to the variety. An elderly woman is standing beside her bike, she's wearing a floral blouse, her hair crammed inside an ill-fitting helmet. She looks up and down, wondering if she can cross. She's probably worried I'll take off at top speed as soon as she sets foot on the asphalt.

I wave her across. She gives an ungracious acknowledgement and keeps an eye on me after stepping off. I wonder if she noticed she was being filmed.

I don't know why I chose this village. It could have been any. I just felt an urge to park the car, take the camera out of its case, and capture the moment. To preserve a few traces of the journey. I learned early to trust that kind of intuition, to stop on impulse, even if I found only worthless material. My archive of these whims often proves useful, just when I least expect it. So for no reason I'm filming an unfamiliar village and anonymous passersby. I wish I could see Sainte-Marée again with such a fresh eye.

I'm Dorothée at her destination. And everything she couldn't film of her first meeting with Rose.

Rue Drolet: lines of parked cars in their hundreds, trees keeping watch, recycling bins scattered along the swollen sidewalks, houses crammed unevenly together, their facades disfigured by a continuous network of slender, tortuous, wrought-iron staircases.

It's a long walk to Rose's apartment from the car, which is giving off the smell of burning oil. Take time to linger over details. Here and there, beside the street, are discreet images of the Sacred Heart and a few saints, ceramic mosaics set into the brick fronts of the houses that are packed in a solid wall. A clump of pansies squeezed between two slabs of concrete. A tiny square of grass adorned with a few sprightly annuals.

I set foot on the grey steps and grasped the too-low railing. With my bag over one shoulder I thought of Rose Brouillard, who has to climb this staircase every time she comes home, when the summer rainfall on the steps has made them slippery, or when the frigid winter sun has turned the slightest snowfall into an icy hazard. For the first time I imagine Rose as a nervous old woman who might refuse outright to see me.

I take a few shots from the veranda. In Montreal, with its one-way streets boxed in between compact blocks of brick and stone, sky is rare and there's no horizon. The poor old woman must have felt really down the day she moved into the city, always wanting but unable to see into the distance.

People who have never been possessed by the horizon never miss it. But when you've been imprisoned by it for so long you must be struck by its absence whenever you meet with a brick wall, whenever you turn a corner, after every intersection you cross.

I'd have liked to film our meeting some other way. To have made it more than a simple interview. To make a film, a real one, about her and her life, one that people could watch onscreen. But as usual I didn't dare. It was for fear of bursting a bubble, of silencing her, as if my camera (she called it the "picture-taker") could stop up her mouth, allowing nothing out or in.

The picture I have: the old woman from too close up. Her face, which I sometimes lose when she leans forward, when she comes closer or draws back. I can't see that she's sitting in her kitchen, but I can guess.

I can't see the wooden table and chairs, the beam in the middle of the room, the four walls, the counter – a tiny one, the battered appliances, the little scraps of paper stuck all over the walls and on things, the window, clouded by a film of moisture. I can't see the window, but I can see the old woman occasionally looking through it. Or, rather, I see the old woman looking at it. For she can't see through.

Actually, I only see her face as a blur – when she doesn't vanish entirely.

I'm Rose. At last. I'm Rose, while her memory continues to be threatened by the gravest disappearances.

So that's how you become a character. Some young woman turns up unannounced and asks you to tell her your story.

Some people do turn up unexpectedly: illegitimate sons who get the urge to appear on the doorstep of the paternal home; apprehensive lovers dreading the thunderbolt of a rejection; politicians with outstretched hands, eager to shake yours; religious folk, salespeople, victims of accidents, folk who are lost. Lost folk.

Sometimes I get lost. When that happens I sit down on the porch of a nearby house, or I knock on the door. Usually, they help me find my way.
　　I'm lost again. Concentrate! I must concentrate better.

As I was saying, that's how you become a character. When a young woman comes into your home, sets up her camera, and calculates aloud the distance, the light, the ambient noise, the white balance, and so on. When she comes and sits down in front of the cup of tea that was probably meant for her, sits down and gazes at you. When she asks her questions, a whole list of questions, about everything and about nothing at all.

I'm Dorothée, with her mouth full of the questions that have bothered her since the start of the project.

Your name is Rose Brouillard, isn't that so? You're really Rose Brouillard, I can't believe it, it's truly you, Keeper Onile's daughter. The daughter from the headland. The daughter from the island. Rose. Brouillard.

Another switch: I'm Rose, testing out her own name.

That name. With its distant smell. Its smell of the place I come from. That name that isn't altogether mine.

It took me a long time to get a name. It required the mainland. And the Bourgeois of Sainte-Marie. And even after all this time my soul still doesn't take to it. There's no one to call me by it, anyway.

Rose Brouillard.

Rose from the headland.

Rose from the island.

Like they said. The mainland folk. The ones on the coast. The village folk.

When you're alone, when you live alone in a story you share with your father, you've no need of a name. When you share your life with Onile, the Keeper and the papa in the story, a name's no use. If one of you says something, the other one hears, there's no need for names, and it's fine that way.

It's true that Onile, the papa in my story, was sometimes called Papa. Naturally. And, also Monsieur Onile, rarely. That was when some other man came on the island. Someone Onile had saved, one of the ones he went to fetch off the open sea. Or the delivery boy carrying his box on his shoulder or in his arms, laden with our order. But I wasn't called anything. I'd go and hide when some man came ashore. And Onile would just wait till I came back of my own accord. In those days I was never called anything, I never needed a name.

Or maybe Onile would sometimes call me Child. Or Little One. Or Daughter. On evenings when he'd been drinking a little too much and became talkative, at times like that he'd call me Little One when he spoke to me. As if it was spelled with capital letters.

Little One.

He'd pronounce it carefully. And I liked that. He'd say, Little One, come to your papa, come child, come onto your papa's knee, and then he'd tell all kinds of stories, stories of the sea, and he'd sing songs, songs of the sea, that I'd listen to, me, his child, me, his daughter, closing my eyes to savour the moment, Little One, falling asleep in his arms, one ear against his heart, off somewhere else inside my head.

Questions pour from Dorothée's lips. She wants to tell my story, my whole story, to the people who will visit the headland, the island. She calls it Keeper's Island.

My whole story.

Where Rose's story is concerned, Marguerite is better informed than anyone. So I've become Fleur, or Flore, or Florence, who has rarely seen her Marguerite display such enthusiasm.

Marguerite knows such a long piece of Rose Brouillard's story. Having had to look for her address has given her back her good humour. I should mention that she was one of the first in the village of Sainte-Marie to know about the little girl on Keeper's Island.

In those days Marguerite was like other girls of her age, suffering no more heartache than the others, with just as many dreams in her head, and with a young woman's desires.

In those days Marguerite had a beau. This was young Bourgeois, whose father kept the general store and did business with the folk on the nearby islands. When the boy turned eighteen he'd already been going to sea for a long time, making deliveries with his father. For more than ten years or so. He knew the job, the people, the river, the risks, and all the good deals to be made. Now, all alone on the boat, he could go wherever he liked, taking different routes. That's how he saw the child.

The Bourgeois boy, when he was in the village, would make deliveries out our way. He'd ride his bike, with a basket attached to the handlebars. He'd stop in front of the house, looking as if butter wouldn't melt in his mouth, and take two or three turns across from the veranda, pretending to be worn out from riding up the hill, and whistling for a bit to attract attention.

Marguerite, at fourteen, contrary to what you might think, was the brighter of the twins, so she was always first outside. That's how Bourgeois the son recognized her. As soon as he saw her dashing out through the open door he'd call her name: Marguerite! Then he'd get off his bike to accompany the twin who'd joined him for a little stroll along the pathway of trodden earth.

Right there in the open, over about fifty yards, he'd make her laugh, tickle her ribs, and whisper smut in her ear. It was she told me about the smut. Maybe she was fibbing. But I remember she'd laugh. He never left content unless he'd heard her laugh.

Except that day, after he saw the girl on the island for the first time, it was different. He'd taken his bike when he got back to the dock, but instead of returning to the shop to see his father he came straight to our house. He whistled.

Marguerite had recognized him and understood something was up, for it was unusual at that time of day: he didn't usually make deliveries at nightfall. In spite of the dark and the gossip it might inspire, Marguerite went out to meet him at the corner of the house. Mama, in a fine fury, swore she'd never allow Marguerite to leave the house again. And that's how it was until the spring tides.

But she'd gone out that evening; Mama hadn't been able to keep her in. And it was that evening he told her. About the island child. The child that was born along with the rumour, the rumour that would start to spread from that evening on.

Born at the age of ten.

I'm Rose, turned inward, into her fuzzy world. But a lucid Rose, who understands a little, who understands she has nothing to understand, who's trying – that's it – who's trying to understand.

It's certainty that evades you first, that defies you, and is lost. You know things by the way you feel them. It's a felt knowledge. It's not that I forget. It's that I'm in all of my life at the same time.

I'm a multiple-choice existence.

Small a: I'm myself, but myself as a young woman, already mis-shapen, but proudly so, with work-worn hands, sweat on my brow, facing life the way I face work, never tiring. I envy the city women, the erect ones, the ones who never limp, the ones Mama told me about when I was small.

Small b: I'm today, a day rather than a woman, an old day that stretches on, worn out, with a stale odour. Or maybe an old woman weary of her day and her silence. Or maybe an old silence.

Small c: I'm a little girl, with grazed knees and elbows, dirty hands and face, my feet or eyes in the water, absorbed, looking everywhere but straight ahead, as if sniffing the wind, following it – it and nothing else. I'm a little girl, shy when a visitor comes, hiding, not wanting to be seen, and I watch those foreign bodies from afar, those manifestations of life, those strange beings.

Small d: None of the above. Because sometimes I just *am*, I simply *am*, disconnected from everything, from the world around me. I merely *exist*, I'm a presence. A present. Something apart. Yes, it's true, it's not good to be so cut off from the world. It's painful. Fortunately, it's rare, but increasingly less so.

When it's small d, I become a body in performance, an empty choreography. At times like that I wait for it to pass. I see myself: my body seated at the table, alone; my body standing at the window with a fragment of the world in view – not always the same one, not always the right one; my body sitting in the living room, alone; then standing at the kitchen counter, still alone; then stretched out on the bed, in the half-dark, on my back, like the corpse of a dead woman, the corpse of me dead, hands on my belly, wearing a peaceful smile, like a dead woman, not a sleeping one, though with no sad expression, all alone; I'm an old woman who feels like a corpse before my time, without any mourners to sprinkle my inanimate remains with tears and fragrances, to wail in despair at my passing, to try to revive me with a slap, to bang a fist on the lid of my invisible coffin.

At other times it's still small d: none of the above. But that's because I can be what I'm really not. I become something else, or differently. There's no explaining it. It's not something I desire. It just happens. There's no escaping it. A rare ecstasy in my lonely old woman's life. When that happens, my whole existence becomes concentrated. I'm enveloped by everything I've been, everything

I've read, everything I've said, everything I've been told. I see it all clearly. But I no longer possess that timeline that's supposed to organize events and things.

They say that on some Pacific island there's a people with no history, a people that never tells its own story. I heard about it on the radio. For it was described in a book, a well-written book, it seems. Above all, written by someone good. They're a very small people, tiny, shrimpy, but unique, with neither past nor future – not because they haven't lived and not because they have no living left to do, but because they can't think about anything except what they're experiencing right then, about what they are at that moment, what they're thinking at that moment, loving at that moment. No promises, nor expectations, nor disappointments, nor worries.

I'm that people. Don't come telling me I'm sick. I'm an island in the Pacific, and a Pacific island can't be sick. I'm a sun-soaked island. An island that's never been devastated by wars, never consumed by voracious, rising tides, one that has never *been*, period. I'm a people with no mouth, with no words for *yesterday* or *tomorrow*. Just: *I am, I'm going, I'm smiling, I'm alive, I'm dancing, I am, I'm shivering, I'm crying, I'm singing, I'm eating, I am. I am.*

Don't come telling me I'm sick. I'm the present. I'm not each accumulated breath. I'm a full, complete breath, one that endures, never the same, yet never different.

I'm a breath. This breath.

Listen to how I draw in my breath.

Listen to how I breathe out.

And again.

What's the difference between past and future? We think we know one better than the other, but both escape us. Think otherwise and it's even worse.

We can all name the poison that'll kill us. Mine is time. Because it no longer has any consistency, no longer inspires me with any confidence. It's like a panic-stricken horse that bolts, that kicks, that whinnies. It's a horse with the bit between its teeth galloping in my gut. It's a horse of foam, a fluid horse that seeps through all my cracks, welling up like the stormwater that streams off an island, reshaping it.

One day there'll be too much of it in my veins. Time will have infected all my fluids. Polluted everything I have in me. So much will pour out through my every orifice that I'll be totally drained. It's inscribed in my genes. I'm a leaky bag of flesh. One that's running out of time. When you've no memory, nothing sticks.

I'm the Bourgeois son, the delivery boy, when he discovers the island child. It's slack water, just before ebb tide; there are the eider ducks, the seals, and so on.

The weather's perfect. It's high tide. No need to hurry.

At high tide I can get closer to the island. I'll see the feather ducks. They really kick up a racket this time of year, it's quite something. Monsieur Onile must have gone to get some nice feathers for himself. He'll give me some when he's settling up his order. There'll be about eight pockets full. In the village they'll buy the lot.

I'll sell his feathers for him in the village. They clean them up and stuff pillows with them. Eiderdowns too, for the winter. My mother makes lined quilts and puffs up the squares with Onile's feathers. It's nice and warm.

At the western point I slow down. It's on account of the shallows, but it's to see the ducks too, the biggest around here. As much as six or eight pounds sometimes. Running slow, the engine's clatter becomes rounder, and the hull makes fewer eddies in the water. I don't want to risk scaring off the birds. There's no hurry.

Onile leads a strange life. Choosing to settle on an island like he did, far from everyone. But when I think about it I can understand. I've seen folks like that before, all alone on the islands, when I went with my dad on his rounds. I met a lot like him that way. On the islands. In the lighthouses round about. They're people all the same. Now it's me that goes to sea on business, I think I understand him even better than before.

Some seals have collected on the shore, to the south of the island. They're kicking up a racket too. They're drying off. Puffed up in the warm sun. There's fifteen good-sized ones stretching out their flippers, making obscene gestures that'd damn your soul to hell.

On the other side there's cattle gathered, and a little farther east something else moving catches my eye. I cut back my speed, just a little, but the engine gives a belch, chokes, and dies. Lifted up proud just a minute ago, now *La Marchande* slows down, gently buries her nose in the water, and wallows.

It was a child I saw.

There's a child on Keeper's Island! Like a savage, with a skinny little chest, bushy hair falling matted over her face, her skin tanned by the early summer sun.

There's a child on Keeper's Island! She must be eight, or ten, she's like little Florence. An island child, that's never been off it. Unbeknownst to everyone. So Onile's wife must have given him a daughter!

The little thing's squatting on the shore. She's wearing nothing but shorts. She's dabbling in the water with one end of a stick.

I'm Rose, among the eddies. With water all around. There's Onile, anxious. His big, reassuring body.

There's water all around me. All around. Something's wrong.

When I feel panic gripping me like this, when I don't understand, I sit down. I wait. Usually it passes and it all becomes intelligible again.

So I'm sitting here, with water all around. I'm waiting to understand. It's all right, there aren't any waves. I'm not on the peninsula.

I'm Rose moulding herself to her child's body when the river trapped her. She's caught between two ages.

The river is enfolding me. My feet are planted on the stony beach. Tiny shrimp are teeming in a pool, in the water collected there after the last tide, in the space hollowed out between two layers of sedimentary rocks folded back by the geological buckling.

It's a strange dance, with all those feet flailing. I can still see them. I can see them somewhere between my mind and the water spreading around me. Like a rising tide.

A wave came on the peninsula, catching me unawares, suddenly real because it splashed me, chill. And then the panic: a surge of warmth, like a bubble rising into your head.

With my chest puffed out I had to plunge into the icy water. To get back to shore. Through the strong waves. A child's body pushed about, carried farther, thrust under, feet and elbows grazed, a child's body tossed, pushed, and pulled.

The body remembers: I'm icy cold.

My child's body, pushed and pulled, pulled and pushed. Pulled. Pulled by Keeper Onile, the papa of the story. He'd become worried.

When I opened my eyes: his shirtless, soaking body, standing between the sky and me, hands on knees, spluttering, his face dripping with salt water and with tears, tears disappearing into his moustache to be wiped away with the crook of an elbow. And all about him a halo of landscape, the cliff like sharp rows of shark's teeth, the house rising behind his shoulder, Onile the father, overcome.

I'll never forget. That picture, and the sensation. At last, firm ground under my numb body. Waves that are gone, but for the sound. The smart of my grazed knees and my feet, bleeding and dirty. And the cold. A cold that sends you to sleep.

The body's memory again: I'm exhausted.

Then Papa getting a hold of himself. Holding me. His long hands on my shoulders, enfolding them. Papa shaking me, undressing me, holding me against him. Twinges of embarrassment, reminding me I'm conscious. My budding breasts against his chest, my almost naked body that he hugs and warms, that he wraps in his arms again, carrying me up the path to the house. Papa stumbling in the sopping maws of his heavy leather boots. Finally, my body wrapped in an old red blanket of itchy wool, in front of the fire that's lit in the stove despite the warmth of June.

Onile muttering as if mumbling a rosary. Little by little, his empty words swell with meaning:

Promise me this.

Promise me.

That you'll never do that again.

Promise me.

That if you think you're caught by the tide.

You'll sit down.

And wait.

Promise me.

That you'll stand up and wait, with your feet in the water.

That you'll keep waiting.

Promise me that.

That you'll never let yourself panic again. Often it's not the sea that pulls you under, it's the fear.

Promise me you'll sit down and wait till the tide and the panic pass. Just pretend you're a lighthouse and lift your arms skyward. Just make a sound like a foghorn: make a round, round mouth and cup your hands like a megaphone.

A wail: Onile starts to wail into his hands, clasped as if holding a tube.

I'll hear you.

Onile wails again to dispel the fog. I'll come. I promise.

The wailing again, strangely piercing, from between Onile's long, bunched-up hands. Perhaps from mine too, raised before my face.

Promise me.

My ears and mouth are full of Onile's wailing.

> **I'm Rose, back where she was sitting, in her apartment. There's still water.**

The peninsula is joined to an island, the island to an archipelago, the archipelago to a thinning fog. Everything's fine, there aren't any waves. I'm not on the peninsula. There's no rising tide.

I'm sitting in the kitchen, with water all over the floor around me. It's no use waiting for Onile, he won't come. The water on the ground is from an overturned bucket.

I'm alone. I must have made this mess myself. I was washing the floor, most likely. There's water everywhere. There's the mop, lying behind my chair. I just need to swab. Wring it out over the bucket. Swab again. Wring it out again. Then empty the bucket into the washbasin. And put the mop to dry outside, on the veranda. The veranda that overlooks . . . I don't remember what.

Through the window all sorts of landscapes are possible. I've accepted that for a long time now. In my eyes, the world is unstable. And behind it are only the jumbled stages of my life gathered into a foggy archipelago of presence. My life, my awareness, is reduced to a long navigation between islets of treachery. My boat is taking on water, and there's only myself to bail it out. I never can tell if I'm touching bottom, if my feet are on the shingle or in the silt. It's mostly no use trying to find out. So I keep on walking, or I sit down.

I'm a barely emergent archipelago. A barely emergent life. Things come and go in tremorous wavelets. It all covers me, bowls me over. Then the surf pulls back, the water subsides, laden with sand, seaweed, and wrack, carrying it all away, leaving only a deposit of clay at the foot of the marker set up by my father, and a new configuration, new contours, as it withdraws. I'm different each time. The tide has always changed my face.

I exist, changed by the tide. By every tide.

No one likes to appear confused. When I'm no longer certain, I look elsewhere to hide it. When Dorothée came, I looked out the window.

I looked at the window. That window onto every possibility.

I'm Rose renaming the person who has come to ask her questions on their first meeting.

The young woman appeared before me. She was there suddenly, the way a poem you've read in your childhood comes back to you, bringing with it all the dark-skinned beauty of Baudelaire's *Fleurs du mal*. She told me her name; I forgot it. For me, she has always been Dorothée. She's Dorothée, the African girl. Baudelaire's cat. A cat coming straight from my bookshelves.

It's all right to give someone a new name when you've a head like mine. And a memory like mine.

Give a new name – you have to.

Dorothée passed through my apartment as if it had all been written in advance. I'd no idea she was coming, but I had tea for two and a second cup waiting on the table.

Maybe it was all prearranged. Of course, it must all have been arranged.

> **I'm Dorothée, listening to the woman who has given her a new name. Rose's world re-emerges, fed by those pictures taken by a long-dead photographer. On the table between the two women, the strangeness of hands meeting.**

I don't like to hear myself speak. That voice that's so unlike me. Above all, I didn't know how to begin. I've been looking for Rose so long that all the questions I've thought of since I signed the contract were waiting impatiently for me to ask her. But I restrained myself, teeth clenched in a smile that I hoped would seem friendly. First, I'd have to earn her trust.

Anyway, finally seeing her made some of my questions less urgent. There was something else. It was the way she welcomed me without asking why I'd come. That second cup on the table. As if someone had announced my visit before I arrived. Maybe Vigneault the sacristan. Or one of his spinster cousins who perhaps couldn't wait to spread the news of my visit.

One thing at a time. First, let me explain to her.

Between our two bodies face to face there's a wooden table, the irritating tick-tock of the clock, and the suddenly warm air, and on the table, in the warm air, the cups, the teapot, and the doughnuts dusted with icing sugar. Also, a pile of yellowing pages I'd laid there, and an old notebook in a thick leather cover, an ancient volume that had been brought here the same way, with tenderness and care.

Suddenly, something happened. Thanks to the video I can tell the exact moment, to the nearest second. It was something in the old woman's face, in her eyes maybe, in that almost imperceptible movement of her body. You could suddenly sense what had burst into the little apartment along with me and the notebook: a wind off the sea, laden like a carousel of confused images about to revolve under a play of floodlights. The island, the headland, and the house. The horizon, brought closer by the fog. A yellow motorboat tracing its furrow of white broth through the river waves. A nervous hare. A flock of terns hailing down on the rough waterz. A green, pink, and mauve sunrise on the distant line of the gulf. The woodshed. The rowboat. The white sheets.

The white sheets hung out on the line. To dry. To be bleached by the sun and absorb the smell of the sea. As if more was needed than the whiff of ozone that floods the house as soon as a door opens, or a window, as soon as eyes open to a new morning. Those white sheets are there, floating, to steal the fragrances of the landscape. Then the bed, smelling of it all.

And even more images that flit by too quickly, escaping us, until the wind-blown carousel is empty and all that remains is light that fades before Rose's eyes. All in a single instant. I'll have to remember that in the editing. That instant. Those images.

Over the years this old notebook with its thick leather cover has contained more than words: dust, the salt moisture of the open sea, of time. It's a sponge of a notebook, its pages swollen and waffled.

Before the woman's weary, hesitant gaze, there's no stranger anymore. Nor anyone familiar, whose name she may simply have forgotten. There's no more table, no more tea, no serving plate; around her there's no more kitchen, nor door opening on the alley, nor window unable to reveal a landscape that isn't initially in the mind. Now that world exists for just one thing: a notebook that appears out of nowhere, out of a nowhere that still lingers inside her head, out of that gaping void behind her forehead, behind her eyes.

The notebook is resting on another table. No alley is visible through that liar of a window. There's a fog, a fog that grows thicker as the old woman's hand approaches the black leather cover. Touching it gently. Feeling its smoothness beneath her fingers. Picking it up.

Inside, a familiar handwriting.

Then, my explanations. I tell her about the work on the Keeper's house, the redecorated walls, the restored inner walls, the replaced floorboards, the floor sanded and soaked with tung oil. And I tell her about all the treasures discovered there, including these letters, this heap of yellowed pages. I leaf through them as she watches. Even if they contain hardly anything, just run-of-the-mill messages exchanged with a few village folk, they're beautiful to look at.

Explanations too about the dilapidated writing desk. I tell her about opening the front lid. About all its pigeonholes and drawers that were emptied of an assortment of objects. A pocket watch. With a boat engraved on the back. An empty cigarette box. The handful of square-headed nails. The fountain pens. The cards. The newspaper cuttings. The sticks of charcoal. The sketches. The plans. The black notebook. Along with other notebooks. All left there since Rose's departure. Since the even more sudden departure of Keeper Onile.

I tell her I've read them all. To learn the story, the history of the house and of the people who lived there. I tell her it's my job. That I've read everything. I tell her: the tiresome descriptions of landscapes. The delivery boy's visits. The painstaking inventories. The plans to renovate and build. The work on Onile's boat. The garden, the growing plants, the fine plans for the buildings, the losses, the harvests, the fishing, the drying, the accounts. I tell her the smallest details, the ones she already knows.

Then those photos we found in the house on the headland and elsewhere, photos we'll soon be sending to the National Archives, and that I spread out on the table in front of her.

First photo: Keeper Onile standing, wearing overalls and a long-sleeved white sweater, his glass to one eye, scanning the horizon, leaning against the corner of the house to steady himself.

Second photo: in overalls and white sweater again, and knee-high rubber boots, one hand on the railing with its balusters of St. Andrew's crosses. Behind him the sky is just as it always seems in photos from those days. The weather must have been glorious – full sunlight, blue sky, and a warm breeze. You can see that his sweater is clinging to his body.

Third photo: this time sitting on the rocks beside the sea in overalls and a warm jacket, rubber boots and floppy beret, holding a still-empty basket, on his way to harvest from the garden.

Other photos: by the boat, on the jetty; in the house beside the Bélanger stove; always standing or sitting, a little stiff, staring at the lens with the same put-out expression and a forced smile.

Rose Brouillard doesn't remember everything. But she does remember the photographer. He came specially on account of the Keeper, a hero who used to rescue fishermen. On account of his solitary life too. With Papa Onile reluctant to act the part, posing here and there, going through the appropriate motions each time, following the instructions of the picture-taking expert who was saying: Do this. Do that. A little more like that. Onile who had asked the child to stay hidden. She doesn't remember why.

But she does recall the photographer, she certainly does, she repeats it, she's categorical. With his picture-taker that he held against his belly and his bent head, going about his job. And all the paraphernalia he carted along the headland paths, on the jetty, on the boardwalk along the bank, around the house, on the boat, and wherever he could put them down. She remembers the photographer, his smooth face, his baggy eyelids, and his right ear. It had two lobes. You don't forget an ear with two lobes.

The old photos are passed across the table between my young hands and her tired ones; the little phalanx of her thick, misshapen index finger strokes the picture, and then back they come to my fingers. Then Rose Brouillard's attention shifts gradually from the laid-out photos to the hands moving around them.

She tells me, Sometimes I don't recognize my hands anymore. That it's worse when they encounter hands as perfect as mine. She's fascinated by my black hands with their pink palms: she turns them over, touches them for the first time. She complains about her hands, long misshapen from the needlework and then from threading the machines. She complains about her yellow nails, consumed by lunules that are turning blue.

You have really beautiful hands, she tells me. I wish I'd said the same to her. Her old hands are magnificent.

I should have filmed them.

Then we return to the notebook, the one so different from the others. The black one. In which it's written about a woman coming. And then about a child. She was the mother in the story. And then the daughter in the story.

That was you, Rose, I told her. You. The daughter in the story.

And then, that clumsy question: I'd like to know about it, to know your story. So that I can tell it to the people that will come to visit the house on the headland. So that I know about your life, and about the people in it.

The old woman, the Keeper's daughter, begins to laugh till she coughs, and then laughs even louder. That was clumsy of me. Listening to the sequence again, I feel the same discomfort. But it's such a lovely moment, watching her and hearing her laugh.

I'm a skeptical Rose, scoffing.

There's nothing on that headland. Trees, a river, a handful of shingle, a peninsula that likely no longer exists. A house surrounded by nowhere. No one will want to go there.

I'm Dorothée, who knows about tourists.

If only she knew. In Sainte-Marée-de-l'Incantation there are already lots of tourists. The company that hired me would never have sunk so much money into it if the region wasn't already deep in profit's shadow. You had to see Jérôme's expression, the bearded guy in charge of the paperwork at the office, when he saw the figures about the number of visitors: a stunning increase over the past few years. He went on for almost an hour about the economic

33

spinoffs, the partnerships to be created, the question of supportive development, and so on. He wanted me to be able to talk about it to make sure the locals would co-operate.

It's true that the village of Sainte-Marée is a historical jewel. It's as if everything had converged on it, as if everything of interest had accumulated there. And Rose still doesn't know, maybe she'll never understand the whole truth, but she's part of it. In spite of herself. Just because she existed.

Tourists come to Sainte-Marée, whatever she thinks. Even though they still know nothing about her.

Tourists are strange creatures. They're not easy to characterize. They come from Quebec City, sometimes Montreal. Maybe Villeray, who knows? They may have met Rose before I did, without knowing who she was.

I've seen tourists who know nothing of the world except their own neighbourhood and their way to work. That kind are out of their element, impressionable. Then there are the ones who've been to Cuba, or Paris, or even China with its modernized villages; you find that, now that people travel packed into buses from which they pour like an excited herd of cattle. They can be one or the other, they may have seen all kinds of places. But whatever their knowledge of the world, you have to be able to maintain their constant interest. And that's not easy.

I sometimes imagine one, and try to put myself in the tourist's shoes as he looks for his own little corner of the world along the river. One that's going back to something, as if to his origins, with a homing compulsion he can scarcely understand. One he often only follows by instinct.

I'm inside the head of a new character. He's a flyfisher. Around him there's a diffuse presence, one that will succeed in making a tourist of him.

we're off on a trip, leaving today, she tells me, like it's a done deal, I woke up inside her, her body, that had surreptitiously straddled my dick, which was getting hard near the end of my sleep and from the hormones she gives off, and her body, her naked body stretched out beyond me, eyes closed in the half-shadow of her concentrated face, her white skin speckled with a few russet spots, all to give me the impression I'm her pedestal, the pedestal of a sculpted nymph like the ones that sashay about, immobile in every corner of Paris.

the surprise came with her abrupt movements, I woke inside her, mumbling, still furry-tongued, muttering something unintelligible, and her right hand moved from my pedestal shoulder pinned to the bed to my mouth,

she covers it gently, my mouth, letting a stream of air whistle between her teeth, between her soft lips, shhh, don't say anything, and I'm rocked by the pounding of her hips, and she opens up,

we're going on a trip, leaving today, she repeats, like it's an established fact, never letting up her motion, it's decided, she tells me again,

I'm the pedestal of a statue about to collapse,

there she is upright on my body like on a barricade of flesh, making her claim, taking possession, on my barricade body,

she, on the hecatomb of my body, a sheet drawn up over one shoulder, her breast spilling from the folds of cloth, a Marianne ready to call for liberty, equality, and fraternity,

equality my ass, oh yes, she's gotten the upper hand all right,

and there she is, bent in the arch of her triumph, an icon in its niche, radiant, gently massaging my scrotum with supple fingers, an arm slipped behind her back to allow her hand to pass below her buttocks, her wrist a gentle pressure on my perineum,

so I say, Pardon? the way people do when they want to be sure they've understood something they'd rather not have heard,

I ask her, Pardon? like you do when you know you've got to ask, but haven't the slightest desire to find out,

then she lets her naked body fall backwards, between my outspread legs, and then, facing *The Origin of the World*, I fall apart,

what a morning can be born from between her thighs, what a morning to be born between her thighs, but what a morning!

she informs me we're setting off this morning, that the bags are packed, that's what I stumbled over in the dark getting up to pee all the red wine she made me drink last night, all the red wine she made me drink, now I get it, for fear I'd set off to fish in the wee hours of the morning, all the red wine that gave me this dry mouth and sore head, me wanting to take advantage of this time with the children away to get some fishing in, and dammit, there goes my week's fishing down the drain, what a morning can be born from between those thighs,

but what a morning can be born from between those thighs!

I'm the flyfisher-become-tourist, after lovemaking.
He'd like to be told the destination.

Squatting after two bouts of lovemaking, my Marie is delicately sponging away the fluids that have flowed into her body (and from it). I'm talking at her back that she's rounding, her head bent forward in the posture – an unlovely one, it has to be said – that she always adopts. That's how I love her. Not necessarily naked, I mean, just a little raw, a little gauche; nothing dramatic or affected, not always primed to be lovely, but just the way she is, with no calculation. So that's it, I talk at her rounded back, eyeing the curve of her ass, she's not looking, so I take the opportunity, and as she's finishing wiping away the excess, I ask, So where are we off to?

I'm Marie, the angler's lover. She answers him.

Sainte-Marée-de-l'Incantation. It's at the end of the road, or almost. A road they've paved just recently. Finished a few years ago. It'll be inspiring.

I'm the flyfisher again, having been told his destination. The children are away at summer camp, but you have to think of them.

Give me a break! There can't be any such place as Sainte-Marée-de-l'Incantation.
Or else it's true: almost the end of the road.
Marie had been preparing her coup for a good while; she had a brochure all ready to convince me, a few stapled pages with a

description of the village. You work up the tourists with photos of rivers and sunsets, women with bare shoulders and their hair tied up in spotless towels getting a massage from men in green coats, and flowers, lots of flowers, and paintings of animals. It's publicity for a little village that was nothing before the road finally reached it: Come and discover the unique, incomparable story of Sainte-Marée-de-l'Incantation – an invitation accompanied by three exclamation marks.

I'm Rose again, collecting her memories. Also, her entire story summarized in a list.

She wants to tell my story to the tourists who'll come. She wants to know about the different characters in it.

Characters. That's what you become when you look like me. When there's no time anymore. When you've lived it out, your time. When it's leaking through every pore of your skin.

Characters. All the characters in your own story. Everything I am. In my own head.

There's Onile, the Keeper without a lighthouse, the papa in the story. With his moustache, his floppy beret, his suspenders, and his father's love.

There's Onile's dog: at first she's a puppy, then an excitable dog, then just a dog, then a dog grown too old, then a dead dog buried behind the shed where the wildflowers grow. I'd like to have wildflowers feed on my body after I'm gone. Like Onile's dog.

There's Mama. Sometimes. Not all the time. She's there in my story, but not for very long. She's still there, covered with flowers too – I mean the wind-tossed ones on top of the tall cliff. She's still a little bit there, that's for sure. As long as the cliff has finished dying and has left her up there.

There's the nanny goat in the shed that gives milk and cheese and leaves little round droppings around the shed and farther off. The goat's never tied up. You can't run away from an island when you're a goat. You can't run away from an island.

There's the mare; she's indispensable, indispensable for the

37

firewood, for collecting the wood on the island, indispensable for crossing the ice in winter, sometimes going as far as the village – for Onile has been known to go all the way to the village, not often, but when I was older. In the village she's scared, the mare, scared of everything, of too many people, of children running, and so on. She's indispensable, that big mare with her twitchy nose all bristled with coarse hairs, and her globous eyes that always look so sad.

There are the cats in the shed. They sleep in the pile of hay in one corner. But I never go near them – even Onile never goes near them unless they come to him of their own accord. Their eyes: scary eyes. But the cats in the shed eat the mice, so it's a good thing they're there. Even if they do have those eyes. Scary eyes. For there are mice. Field mice, with bulging eyes: little creatures that love flour, and nuts, and potatoes, and grain, and meal, and woollen blankets. Their tiny droppings left in the ruined woollen blankets. The fits of anger they can provoke. In Mama's day they rang out loud and clear.

There are the trees. You can hug them. Do you want to? You can. They never flinch. Sometimes they break, but they never flinch. It happened, once: it broke. I fell.

That's the way things are. It really hurts, but you learn. Learn what can be broken by an embrace.

There are the herons.

The cormorants.

The big ducks on the western point.

The razorbills.

The gulls. The seals too. And the porpoises.

Baudelaire's cat is interested in the whales. She wants to know if Onile, the papa in the story, used to hunt whales with the village men. There had to be a few of you to do that. Onile wasn't keen on hunting when there had to be a handful of men.

They're lovely, the whales. Impressive. I never tire of seeing them turn their backs to me. Heading east-southeast. Sometimes they're huge. Other times they're small and white. Their tails that wave to you. I wave back when I'm on the cliff.

The cliffs. There are the cliffs. The little one, but the big one especially.

There's the house, set on top of the little cliff. Or maybe it's the main character. That's what she thinks, Dorothée. For she's come about that house, to find out more about it. It's what casts a shadow over the story. And it casts light too when the night is dark, when there's no moon, almost like a lighthouse with the flame of the lamp wavering inside. A paradoxical character, the house.

Scattered around this house, all over it, are Onile's words: little scraps of paper stuck to this and that with a spot of wax, to teach me to read. Here the word *table*; there, *wall*; and there again, *door*; and nearby, *Papa's room*; on the furniture, *desk*; and, on the flawed windowpanes, words that sometimes lie: *sky, island, veranda, river*. In the morning fog they mean nothing. When the weather's clear, and if I'm sitting at the table, everything's fine: they tell the truth. Yet if I move closer, if I get too close to the words, they lose their meaning: the word *river* is on the veranda, and the *veranda* is lost in the window frame.

Through this window, and everywhere outside, there's the river. It's the only thing that's never lacking. It's always there, on all sides at once. You can't hug it; it does the hugging, it hugs us. It's all around, in front, on the sides, and even in the woods behind. About me, on me, under me, and in me. It's all there is, above all and before all. I know, for I'm nothing beside it. In it, I'm tiny.

Little One. That's what Keeper Onile and the papa in the story calls me when he wants to speak to me. Or child. Or daughter. Did I tell you that? He'd say, Come here, Little One.

He'd say, Eat up, daughter.

When he talked to the dog, he'd call me the child. Watch the child, he'd say. Then the dog would lift an eyebrow, point with her nose, wag her tail, and settle down again.

Also: Daughter, it's time, go to bed.

Little One. Child. Daughter. Little One.

He knows the river, Onile, and has for much longer than I have. He knows you're always little. The river is dumb, but it's deaf too. It's deaf to anger, deaf to misfortune. It never comforts, never cheers. It never did for my mother. It never consoles. Never reassures. Yet, in spite of everything it does give you comfort. It's enough just to look at it. Or lose yourself in it, body and soul. That's the only consolation, sometimes. When you know how to listen to it. With your head in the water, in the deep, muffled sounds of its shifting bed. That's a language very few can decode.

Onile the fisherman, Keeper Onile with no lighthouse, gun, or foghorn, Onile, the papa of my story, he understood all those strange kinds of language. About the weather to come, especially. But about other things too. When you live so long with someone, you use the same words. In the same order. With the same accent. The accent of silence.

With Onile, I'd ended up speaking the same words.

And then Dorothée who asks me with the voice coming from her red mouth and her brown face all aglow: the story.

I'm Dorothée, all ears, not yet satisfied, wanting a lot more.

It's all fascinating, really it is. And if I wanted to tell your story, you know, your whole story, first you'd have to tell it to me in your own way.

Don't you want to tell me your story?

Now I'm Rose, talking too fast, wanting to tell everything the moment she remembers it, her tongue entangled in stories that jostle together, it's like inside her head.

Let me tell her. She wants me to tell her. So here's my story, its main lines and all the others, even the shortest.

There was: the revolution and even Cuba, and Montreal, which is an island and a whole country at the same time, like a continent squeezed into a space inside a bigger continent.

There was: the loneliness – on the island, on the headland, in the water, on the coast, and on all the other islands in the world. Here too. Because in the city too you're alone.

There were: the Russians, the Germans, death, premonitions. There was the love in my innards, from afar, for that delivery boy, a handsome heartbreak. There was the fear in my lungs, a swelling fear, impossible to cry out.

There were: the distant picnics, when folk from the village came to eat on the beach and I kept above, hiding, watching. Their games, my loneliness.

There were: the tides, the birds, their droppings – now that was funny, the gull's dropping on the delivery boy's jacket. That handsome delivery boy. His beautiful hands that brought us everything. His long fingers, so very long. The crate he could carry so effortlessly. And his handsome mouth that you wanted to kiss when he whistled as he climbed the steps to our house. It was he who brought the gramophone to the island.

There was: music. Fortunately, there was music. It hurt Onile, because it thrust an awl into his ears that were still sensitive from an incident that almost left him deaf. Sad. But that music did me so much good.

There were: the days the naked child spent on the shore. Just so old, but older too.

There were: bridges to be built between the islands, to get to the hares, to get to people, to get to a family, a kind of unknown family.

There were: Onile's tears. And his laughter, rare as pearls, scattered along the rosary of the days.

His frame, erect in the storm. His frame sitting at the desk. His frame bent over, threatening. His frame bent the other way, singing, chin up, and his crow's feet. His frame discovered sleeping in unseemly positions: on the boat seat that masqueraded as a bench for the kitchen. Slumped on the table. On the veranda, never feeling the cold. In the doorway, with no discomfort. Lying beside the kitchen table, once too often.

He had sung all night:

> *dondaine laridaine*
> *matapate talimatou*
> *matantalou malimatou*
> *matapate alimatou*
> *matantalo elaridé*

He had sung like that all night till he fell asleep near the kitchen table, once too often that time.

I'm the flyfisher-become-tourist making his final preparations. It's still raining, for three days now.

She put the bags in the kitchen, by the table. She's waiting for me to put them in the car while she goes round the house watering the soil around those green plants she collects and jotting down the usual instructions for the neighbour who'll come in to look after Charles, the family cat.

Without looking at me, she says: It'll do us good. She also says: Your tackle's in the trunk; for sure you'll find time to go fishing.

Time to go fishing, for sure.

And then I think of the kids at summer camp. And I dump every possible worry on her, as if I blamed her for not being more concerned: they're running in the woods and stumbling over roots, hitting one another with branches, pulling one another's hair, tripping one another up on the gravel, rocking the canoes – just imagine it – trying to capsize them and sometimes succeeding, climbing trees, throwing stones at one another.

She tells me to stop, tells me everything will be okay. That she's asked her mother to be available. That she's told the camp to call her mother directly if there's a problem.

But I keep on: they go climbing with frayed harnesses, they hide insects in the others' sleeping bags, or they put hay from the stable in the toilets, or food stolen from the canteen in the baggage, and then they pee on others' mattresses, I imagine if they do that someone will have to go and fetch them.

With a laugh, she asks me to stop. But she throws back at me over her shoulder that they won't do any of those things. Because they take after me.

It's true. They take after me.

I open the door. It's raining. I'm going to throw the bags in the car.

I'm Dorothée in her car, with the windows up, the radio off, and everything that's unfolding in the silence. I'm another man's negress again. Anyway, might as well be in Haiti.

It's raining less than just now. In the kitchen of Rose's apartment the opaque window was half-open. Maybe the sound of the rain dripping on the iron roof of the shed in the back will come through on the recording. But it's not a disaster. Actually, it's quite lovely: Rose's voice, her silences, and rain on the metal.

> *I've been your slave baby*
> *Ever since I've been your way*
> *I've been your slave*
> *Ever since I've been your faith*

Billie has started to sing. As if time had stood still until I started the car again.

I've turned off the radio. In the raw emotion gripping me even Lady Day's voice was out of place. I apologized: Sorry, Billie, I needed some peace and quiet. It's this feeling I have that there's too much noise in my life. I needed the calm purr of the motor, the wipers slithering to and fro, the memories of the interview from earlier piled up densely in my memory. It's difficult for me to grasp the meaning of what has just occurred. Rose isn't telling me her story. She's living it.

It's a thrill we share; her eyes not seeing me, gazing off somewhere else; her hands making mechanical, orderly gestures as they move through the void before her, a void she fills with invisible objects I can sometimes imagine, sometimes not.

She's not telling me her story. She's living it. I'd like that to be obvious on the screen. I doubt I'll be able to. Let me get to the hotel quickly. Watch it again. View it. If Henri gives me time to look.

This evening I'm to meet Henri, the white lover in my story, the one who wasn't willing to go away with me but that I see again whenever I can. Today we're to meet in a downtown hotel that reeks of frying oil, where the sheets and carpet are invariably stained. And where the rooms smell of cigarette ash.

Him.

It's a rather ordinary story. I met him in university. A thirty-year-old guy in a hat I ran into coming out of a building. A lecturer.

I was never his student.

He has no wife to cheat on, as far as I know.

We're not secret lovers. We're just having a short-term relationship. But the short-term stretches on. It's a loop.

The first time we saw each other we exchanged a smile before realizing we were heading for the same metro station. We smiled again, out of embarrassment, then curiosity. And we stopped for coffee. The first evening ended in a brasserie on Saint-Denis, an in place that nevertheless smelled like a sewer. Henri likes places that smell. He says they make you feel more alive.

We met several times. He chose the place. Sometimes it was just in an alley. He'd take me there, under a staircase, from behind, his hand over my mouth, his trousers hardly lowered, before we set off at a run, laughing, him with his belt still loose. And in the fictional bedroom of an apartment empty for the day, an odd, filthy place he'd gotten hold of by offering fifty dollars to some guy begging in the street. At other times treating each other with infinite tenderness during those quiet moments when we took the time to be naked together. In a hotel room, or at my place, where he came a few times.

Henri wasn't willing to go with me when I left for a place that smelled of river, of space, and of forest. He told me he'd suffocate there, that he'd be a dead man walking, embalmed by the flowers and grass. That he'd be bored. The only smells he can bear are oily tar after rain, meat crackling as it turns slowly over the grills of Lebanese restaurants, or the cigarette butts piled up at the base of the facades along Sainte-Catherine. He's an urbanite who could never give up that cluttered landscape. He can only live among humanity. Where it smells of humanity.

If he'd wanted, maybe he could have been something more, something else. But he'll never be anything but my white, big-city lover. If not my almost-friend. For sometimes, above and beyond the romps of our genitalia, we think and talk together. In cafés, on the concrete footpaths in parks, sitting on the steps of Place des Arts, or treading the wooden floors of the local art galleries. If he'd wanted, he could be more. But he's just my white lover and my almost-friend. I don't resent that. He takes me whenever I come back, and that's fine. When I go to him. In some hotel.

Since I left, that's the way it is, in some hotel, with him. I tell him I'm coming on Sunday. He books a room in some smelly hotel, and sends me an email. Telegraph-style:

Hi,
Meet Château Centre-ville.

Or the name of some other hotel, obviously, for we often change the place. Usually he stops at that, and signs off.

When I get there we'll have to make love, I know. Then we'll have to lie there with his lanky frame latched on to mine. All night long he'll take me. He'll make love to me again. Things will start off with his cock against my bare buttocks. The rest of Henri will follow, willingly. Still half-asleep, he'll let go, and take me by the throat, gripping it a little too tight, with sleep as his excuse – it's the excuse I'll make for him anyway: I'll let myself think that sleep has stripped away his inhibitions, summoned up some deeper fantasy; I'll think that what he did was woven into the plot of some dream in which I played no part.

I quite enjoy his firm grip. He becomes aroused faster, spurts, stays inside me, in our juices, and then latches on for another part of the night, always the same bony frame, his arm between my breasts, his palm flat on my collarbone.

I know: I'm his negress.

I know too that it's not me he loves: it's his white hand on my skin. He's already admitted that. But I make light of it, I say: You're my white lover. As if I had others, not so white. That defuses it.

It all means I probably won't be able to look over what I've taped till tomorrow. When I arrive I'll pick up the key at the front desk. That's the plan. In the wan light, a receptionist with a sickly complexion will play queen of the lobby. I'm not going to hang around her desk for her sighs, her rolling eyes, her brusque, imperial gestures. I'll pick up the key card thrown on the desk, go down the corridor in a few rapid strides, and squeeze into the elevator in the nick of time, behind another woman, most likely a hooker, her sex appeal dependent on a collection of garish accessories. And I'll tell myself that the lobby queen I must have dared to disturb probably thought I was one too, a new regular, another whore, a high-class one, who opens her legs for next to nothing, when you think about it, who knows how to tilt her ass just enough, at just the right moment, and to use her mouth and hands all at once. That's what Henri will want from me, anyway. I'll be wanton and sluttish, loosen my body, look him in the eyes, pant a little too hard, put my hand on his balls to feel the spurt when he's deep inside me, to be filled with him, for him to stretch out beside me, for him to enfold me, finally speak to me, so that I know at last, so I can be sure, that the lobby queen was mistaken. So that I know I'm more to him than just his whore. That I also exist for words, for a considered life, one that's thought about, spoken about, reflected on, everywhere about these bodies we'll have rent and conjoined.

I'll tell him about my work there, about my research in Sainte-Marée at the edge of the world and in the surrounding region. How I found myself on rue Drolet, in Rose Brouillard's apartment. How I have to go back there tomorrow. The possibility that she might go there with me, Madame Brouillard. Retrace her steps. Back to that place where he, Henri, was unwilling to accompany me.

A car horn blows behind me. It's on account of the traffic light that's turned green while I wasn't watching. The rain is sluicing off the windshield. As I'm taking off from the intersection, the worn tires of my old Pontiac squeal unconvincingly.

Henri is convinced of a lot of things. He's convinced that the book will outlive all the technological advances, that the big multinationals will devour the world piecemeal, that thanks to racial crossbreeding the true human will emerge, that I should take much more interest in my slave origins.

He knows my skin better than he knows me. He talks to me about the Black Panthers as if I was their legitimate daughter. Tells me in sentences all ending with exclamation marks that the FLQ held training camps alongside the Black Panthers, exclamation mark, some of them anyway, another exclamation mark, that they learned from those revolutionaries, two exclamation marks, from those freedom fighters, exclamation mark, how to lay their bombs in order to change the world with the noise of the explosions, suspension points . . .

He knows my skin better than I do. I've been white all my life. I still am, mostly. When I don't see myself in the mirror. When I don't appear on the screen. When I'm not deep in Henri's gaze. Living among white people has often led me to forget the difference.

Haiti? I've never understood what there might be about me that's Haitian, even for others. I'm sick of all that. Sick of continually being shunted off to somewhere else.

I only know about Haiti from books. Laferrière's, naturally. I found it exotic that there's such a thing as a country without hats. And Roumain's *Gouverneurs de la rosée*, that Henri handed me, saying: You can't claim to know who you are if you haven't read this. I never finished it.

I know Haiti like everyone does, from the obscene disasters they show on the TV news. I got to know the mud, children in the mud. Grown-ups too, young women, young men, older than they'd be if they lived here, like me. The languid amble of this one, his long limbs that speak volumes, his toothless mouth that the cameraman focuses on so carefully because it's so eloquent, so generous with smiles of resignation, so ready to sing, like during the last hurricane when mudslides swept everything away, his son, his daughter, his wife, and all his worldly goods, his mouth so ready to sing again, like each time, like all the others walking in the street, choruses of walking wounded after the earthquakes, with the dust of collapsed walls around their feet.

Haiti's dust chokes me from afar. I prefer the sticky clay at the river's edge to that blackish mud. Mud on a pebble. How could I have any roots planted there?

From a distance, Haiti smells good. For people from here, who come from the cold, it's stimulating to feel the heat. But not with your feet in mud, dreading cholera, living with death, seeing the walking dead, and smelling of filth. Haiti smells good from a distance. It's a nightmare people are always reminding me of. He does too, thrusting my nose back into the pestilence of my forebears' accumulated juices. While I live for air, for water, for open space, and for the wind.

I'm the white lover, in a bedroom, waiting. There's all that has to be ready when she comes.

In the room, my raw body, naked white on the white sheet. Turned low, the pounding rhythm of totally possessed shamans that I put on as soon as the receptionist called to announce the arrival of my guest.

I dimmed the lights, removed my boxers and threw them into the drawer of the bedside table next to the Holy Bible I'd amused myself by leafing through a few minutes before. An undergrad once told me that the Bible could answer all our questions, that we only had to ask: to choose a passage at random, and interpret it. To fill the emptiness of my evening, still dragging on in her absence, I asked the Bible if I could look forward to getting laid tonight. Ecclesiastes provided the answer: without a woman, apparently, a man laments and drifts.

In a few minutes I'll possess her compliant young woman's body to the throb of the ceremonial voodoo chants. I'll possess her body, her eyes turning upwards at the shock of our pelvises.

My hands on her skin, if all goes well. All that to put my hands on her skin.

The door half opens as I expected; she's more radiant than I remembered. I feel chilly. I feel completely naked. I want her to burn me.

She puts her things down on the floor before telling me: You're ridiculous.

I wait, smiling. She'll come all the same. She'll get into bed, call me Henri, even though she knows it's not my real name, even though she knows I borrowed it from the hatter on rue Sainte-Catherine. She'll come over and call me Henri, for sure, and touch me. For she knows how to play the game.

Except this evening that's not how it goes. She pulls the sheet off the other bed in the room and throws it to me. Not letting it fall gently the way you let it float down on the restless little body of a tired child. She throws it to me for me to cover myself, takes her camera out of its case, and then, with the bluish light from its screen shining on her face, lending her skin a purple hue, she views what she filmed during the day, in reverse.

When I get up to join her, taking my time, resigned, gathering the sheet round my midriff, she readjusts the camera slightly to let me appreciate what's happening on the screen. There's an old woman talking. She's badly shot, often left outside the frame. That must be the old woman she was looking for. So she'll be around for a few days.

You found her, I say. There's nothing else to say, she looks so excited in the blue light that lends her more reality than everything else.

She lays the camera on the nearby chest of drawers, and swings her chair around. Her hands slide up my thighs. The shamanic rhythms recapture a little more space in the dimly lit room, a traditional chant from Bali that echoes strangely the electric glow from the touch screen. It won't be the only contrast to be consummated this evening. I run a hand through her hair, poorly straightened and dyed rusty brown. I've never understood why she rejects her origins so strenuously.

Her mouth, her damp-wood lips. She's found me. Tonight, I'll be the one possessed.

I'm Rose, where only her words remain to allow her to exist.

She takes everything with her picture-box. She was most interested in my scraps of paper. They were that nice neighbour's idea. She says it stops you from forgetting. That I need them. So I do what she says: they're little memory-joggers on which I write messages to myself. That way I teach myself to live from day to day. I know

I have to write everything down. Even though I know too that the time will come when I won't be able to read.

I write down everything, all of it.

And I read what I've written. As soon as I come across a little scrap of paper stuck somewhere in front of me, I read it. Often there's no need. Sometimes it's essential. In any case I read, and I do what it says. Just in case I've forgotten what has to be done.

On the frame of the front door of the apartment, at eye level:

Don't forget that I forget.

When I have the impression I'm reading it for the first time, I don't go out. It tells me the fog's too thick for me to venture farther.

Right above it:

If it's raining outside, take the umbrella from the coat closet beside the front door before going out.

And inside the coat closet, right beside the umbrella, I've written:

Wait until I'm outside to open the umbrella.

One day I opened it in the entrance hall. I was stuck there, almost unable to go out, and by the time I managed it, I'd forgotten why I needed to go.

Near the mirror in the bathroom:

I'm an important person.

And near that:

I'm a woman. An old woman. Everything else is past and gone.

Also:

That face in the mirror is me.

It's hard to sum up who you are on a scrap of paper. I was wrong about that last one: *That face in the mirror is me.* I'm not that face. Not at all. Admit that I'm that woman? Those wrinkles? That sagging face? That's never me. I'm on the other side. Somewhere else, earlier, round about.

I'm afraid to take down that scrap of paper, even though I know I was making a mistake the day I scribbled it. The day I take down the messages I've written for myself, maybe I'll be sinking into the salt bog of my memory. Vanishing into the muck like a body thrown off a cliff, tossed about where the water meets the shore, resting precariously on the stones, then slowly slipping back and sinking, covered by the silt that the waves are trying to reclaim from the land.

If I get rid of the words all around me, on which my entire life rests, I feel scared. Scared of dying, of disappearing along with them. So instead of crumpling the paper and throwing it in the wastebasket I read it every time I pass the mirror, and tell myself I was mistaken, that I'm more than that face. That realizing it is another sign that I'm lucid. That I can still recognize myself. I'm still small a, small b, small c, and small d, all those answers in one person.

On the wall, beside the sofa where I usually sit (it's almost a reflex), two messages:

I like to listen to music when I'm reading the paper. To read the paper I have to go and fetch it from the stall in the metro station. The way to it is written on a scrap of paper in the pocket of my coat. The radio is on the bookshelves beside me.

(I put a nice arrow pointing to it.)

And the other message comes next, it's on the bookshelves, above the radio:

Music is good for me. Press here and the radio will come on. To stop the music I have to press the same button.

Sometimes I do the same thing over and over, following to the letter what's written. That's when I can tell it's an empty day.

In the bedroom, by my bed, on the bedside table beneath the lamp:

Mama is dead. So is Papa. I must not look for them. Nor wait for them to come. I must put out the light and close my eyes. I'll go to sleep.

That one makes me sad. Often, I fall asleep only after I've had a cry. Even if I can no longer remember so well who they were, especially her, I do remember the sadness. You don't forget real emotion. It's as if I'd just discovered their lifeless bodies, each on the threshold of its own tragedy, every evening, before bedtime.

There's a post in the kitchen, a kind of Morris column for the house. On this message board planted in my too-tiny landscape, there's a list of my everyday activities:

I must sweep the floor once a day, gather the sweepings into little piles, throw them in the garbage, then put the broom and the dustpan back in the cupboard beside the bathroom, where they're supposed to be.

Also:

I have to take a bath on Tuesdays, Thursdays, and Sundays. The calendar is behind the pantry door, at the end of the kitchen counter.

Last week, or maybe further back, I took two baths on the same day. It was when I was drying myself off for the second time that I realized. The towel was wet. I stood there not knowing what to do, with droplets all over me and water in my creases. The towel was soaking wet. Then my body was almost dry after I waited to find the answer. Problems are sometimes insoluble when you've a head like mine.

Finally, I remembered the other towels. I just had to find them. Then my naked body in the bathroom was ready for a new performance.

My naked body in the kitchen.

My naked body in the passage.

No dry towel.

My naked body in the bedroom.

My naked body in the living room.

No dry towel.

My naked body in the corridor.

Finally, my body completely dry.

I'd simply forgotten, forgotten everything all at once, but especially forgotten what I was looking for. The towels had faded away; my body was no longer naked, or else being naked was no longer a problem.

Then my naked body in the rocking chair. Outside on the veranda overlooking the alley behind the apartment.

My naked body rocking.

Children laughing behind the fence. Mocking laughter. Children chanting. Mocking. If I was all there I'd have recognized that little beast from next door, the one with two lobes to his right ear. And the other two, the redheads who often come to play with him in the alley.

Then that nice neighbour came.

I'm a nice neighbour with her stream of words, without periods, commas, or capital letters, flabbergasted to see Rose's naked body rocking on the veranda of her little apartment and shocked at the children's laughter and jeers, chanting, Naked old woman! Naked old woman! We saw an old woman naked! Like it was a nursery rhyme.

now now madame come come and get dressed

you kids buzz off little brats get going now now madame come and get dressed up you get and don't let me catch you again

come we'll get you warmed up you must be cold let's put on this blouse okay? and you have this pretty jacket and this long skirt will do nicely you've just had a bath is that it? i'll see to emptying your bath take your time getting dressed i'll put your towel on the drying rack or else it'll never dry ·

you

i'm sure you'd like a cup of tea?

I'm Rose, in the whirlwind of her nice neighbour's visit.

She boiled the water, wiped the table and the kitchen counter, and swept the floor. All those things. And she promised me she'd come again. And so she did, often.

The scraps of paper are her, they're my nice neighbour. She's the one who told me to do it. Since she came, Scotch-taped to the kitchen noticeboard there's:

Make tea for two, set two cups on the table with two teaspoons. Then take the doughnuts from the fridge, sit down, and drink from one of the cups while I wait.

She comes every day, often several times in the day, bringing a steaming hot meal. She eats with me. Two or three meals. Leaves me on my own. Comes back. Leaves me on my own. Comes back. Now and again she even tucks me in.

Since she came, the days pass instead of dragging on. Because they taste different. Sometimes it's soup, or broth. Sometimes a meat pie. Sometimes *cipaille*. Sometimes macaroni. Or spaghetti. Chicken. Meatloaf. Stew. Sauerkraut. Or a *bouilli*. Especially towards the end of summer, *bouilli*, like *ratatouille*. For she finds all the vegetables dirt cheap in the market.

Since she came, life tastes of all kinds things. And it's noisy too. It chatters, life does. It's a flood of words whenever her person comes into the apartment, says Hi! puts everything in order, takes her bow, and leaves.

I'm a nice neighbour, a kind of sister-in-law to the Villeray neighbourhood, chatting away to herself in her oversized floral dress, criss-crossing the kitchen, cleaning, serving food, helping to eat, cleaning up again, and then leaving. And life, moulding itself every time to the same chatter with no periods, commas, or capital letters, her talk in the form of a single long paragraph, unbroken, breathless, inexhaustible, and exhausting.

you're feeling great today and at our place everything's great and there's my hubby bertin's cousin who called she's coming to see us it was to let us know she was coming this summer so we chatted you know how it is it had been an age we had all kinds of things to tell each other do you remember her my hubby bertin's cousin i've told you about her before i told you about her already she's the one lives in fort lauderdale i've always had problems with that word *lauderdale* fort lauderdale well yes she's the one married to a truck driver you know the truck driver from the states and she's the one made her money working in a bar for tourists because with her accent from here you know the people liked her a lot the people that came from here that went down to get a bit of sun in fort lauderdale anyway now she's loaded now she's hoarded hoarded hoarded made piles raked it in and now she's loaded so when she comes to see us she always gives us lovely presents last year she gave me a marvellous set of china dishes or anyway it looked like china and it was made there so i think basically it was china with a pretty blue border just exquisite and pretty blue flowers all over i tell you a marvellous thing like always when she gives me presents she gives us something every time she comes when she came the year before last it was a stuffed toy parrot that could whistle when you went past him a real hoot you should have seen it it made me laugh and laugh and i put it in the kitchen so that way when my hubby bertin went to fetch himself a beer you know it would give a whistle the parrot would my word really it was funny tons of presents every time and that's not counting the bottles she brought us good wine from the states she's all heart my hubby bertin's cousin i've brought you one of her bottles from the states to let you have a taste you know you'll see with the stew i've made for you it'll be real good

I'm a hungry Rose sitting in front of a steaming plate and a wineglass waiting to be filled.

Pour me a glass, it'll be good, it's been so long since I drank wine. So long.

I'm the nice neighbour finishing her speech, getting her second wind, adopting her mocking yet caring attitude.

come on now you always say it's been a long time though i brought you some last friday not this one but another bottle look the snow has started up again did you notice? i'm going to have to leave you to your wine rose i'm going back to my hubby bertin before he falls asleep on the sofa

I'm a liar of a window that people try to see through. Then another, in a different place.

An old women flies out through the glass; she sees bits of that white void she's beginning to know so well, that absorbs by allowing the body to subside.

She sees Hare Island, girdled by the river. She sees Mama in her flowered dress, Mama singing, almost smiling.

She sees Onile's dog, still running, somewhere along the shore.

She sits stock-still, slack-mouthed; it's her mind casting itself out the window, as often happens, very often. She'll be back, no need to worry.

Off there, inside the old woman's head, there's that moustache turned towards me. It's Onile's, who people say is the papa in the story.

He sees the veranda, the dock, the horizon.

Then, as he's done for so long, he sees his failure, a tragic failure he couldn't have avoided. And pours himself another glass.

A young woman follows the first, follows the old woman, as if she also wanted to fly out the window.

She follows the gaze of the first, as if she could see the same thing, imagine she's seeing the same thing.

What she sees: an alley, a very ordinary alley, soaked by a July shower, the unexpected kind. The kind that reeks of warm water and the washings off walls and streets. The sort that flows down me, leaving its traces. It's been falling since yesterday, in scattered showers.

Through another like me, a man, slender, sees a downtown boulevard. He's about to make a decision. This evening the hotel room he'd booked will be empty. He flings a book into his bag and leaves the room. It's not the first time that looking through a window has given him the urge to leave.

Here, after a long silence, things are about to start moving again. Since I'm half-open, the two women inside shiver – not that it's cold, it's from the damp I let in. Last week people were hot. They got used to it. Since yesterday I've been letting in the constant gurgle of the eavestroughs and the steady drumming on the corrugated iron. Since that young woman came.

 She stands up, offers to make a fresh pot of tea, runs the tap in the sink before going to fetch the electric kettle from the end of the counter.

Water is flowing. In the streets like in the kitchen.

I'm Rose, gazing into the water, into all the waters, into the river water; and then there's the river's language, while the faucet sobs its melody.

 You don't hear the river water flowing. Tiny brooks chatter noisily – I've heard the babble of some all the way from the mainland. But the river is a long, tranquil silence. Of course it can roar, dash against the shore, tear things loose, lift them, throw them about. In winter it makes quick work of the pack ice, ripping it asunder. In the roughest storms I've seen it shatter the window of the house on the little cliff. A crushed lump of ice turned up in the kitchen, shapeless, among the shards of broken glass. It can roar and destroy, the river can. But you never hear its water flowing. It doesn't flow, it stays. It's a silent rumble. An immobile tremor. It's the still photo of a flame's crackle.

 Baudelaire's cat stretches gently, arches her back with pleasure,
 it's Dorothée,
  she thinks I talk well about the river,
  reaching her arms over the table,
  that I describe it well. And Onile, the papa in my story too.

Her eyes are sparkling. She says that's why she's taking notes and filming. Because I know what's audible. And what isn't.

**I'm Onile saying no, who's not really a keeper, who
may be partly one, but not of a lighthouse.**

They can say what they like. I'm no hero. I've lost too many lives.
And I'm nothing close to a lightkeeper. I know all about it, I know
what a keeper's life is like.

I've lots of time, ahead of me, and in all the compass of my days.
A hundred and twenty hours of work a week, sometimes, for real
keepers in the peak foggy season. When all week the fog robs the
horizon of its place, when you have to crank the foghorn by hand
and keep a watch all round, and sometimes launch the boat, and
wind the light's turning mechanism sometimes three times during
the longest nights, and repair it now and again, and turn the light
by hand till it's over, and go up and down the long stairs again and
again, the hundred and ninety-two spiral steps of the Brandy Pot
lighthouse, I no longer suffer that kind of wear and tear, that stone
cylinder rising up like a needle in the middle of the staircase, the
hundred and ninety-two steps to climb, up and down, up and down,
never puffing or panting, never collapsing, never stopping, never
neglecting the daily duties – waxing the floors, polishing the brass –
or the most urgent repairs, the major maintenance on the building
and the fittings. There's sometimes a hundred and twenty hours of
work a week for real lightkeepers, at the height of the foggy season.
That wasn't for me.

In my life the essential thing isn't the foghorn, or the all-too-fal-
lible mechanism of the lamps, or that endless staircase. Work, yes.
There are times when the whitewash has cracked the skin on my
hands. But apart from that I'm no keeper.

Except for looking out the window. And there, the language of
the river. The reefs foretelling what may be in store, whether things
might turn nasty. That's what it was. That's what made me a bogus
lightkeeper, an amateur, a make-believe one. Yet I'm just a fisherman.

On my knees: my precious wooden box. When I open it
I examine every single tool, like I always do. And my fingers
follow my eyes, lovingly, along the handles, the cutters, the gouge,

the chisels, the scorp, even the wooden mallet. And I remember one windy day, a sunny day. It might have been uneventful. But:

A thirty-knot wind, squalling to forty.

Waves rising to the west. Violent.

An unforgiving hazard. One that can easily snap a boat's propeller.

The same reefs as before, the same as always: deceptive. Or a shoal. The boat getting too close, far too close. Maybe the engine failed. Or the captain didn't see the buoy. Rocking violently.

A distress flare.

In the past I've helped others. In springtime the icefield can be fickle. The blood on the ice isn't always animal blood. When I go to fetch a hunter caught in the ice there'll be hoarfrost on his beard, in his lashes, on his skin. Whether I reach him in time or too late is a matter of chance, of good luck or bad. Once they're rescued they're on their way again, and that's fine.

But that one, the captain of that boat with the broken propeller, he came back to see me a few months later. A German. And he returned every year after that, around the same time. One day when he was here he saw me on the veranda whittling a piece of wood with my penknife. The next year he came bringing me this woodcarver's kit. A thank-you gift. The best thanks I've ever had, by far.

That's all I am: a fisherman, a woodcarver, lucky when I see, sad when I don't. A lookout rather than a keeper.

Another year the German brought me a dictionary, a lovely French-German dictionary. He could see from my library that I could read more than the river.

> I'm Rose just emerging from her fog, sensing she's not alone. Among other things, it's when it was time to set off for the city, where she imagines she'll find a milky scene.

Feeling. I can feel. Returning to reality after a dizzy spell, when everything finally settles down, when order returns, when the chaos subsides. And I'm finally back in my place.

I can feel. Back on solid ground after more than an hour in a whirl.

With the movement around me instead of under my feet. Bodies moving. A hubbub of voices. Life.

So I can feel. Feel like a human. The shock of feeling. Of understanding I'm a human. Maybe you've read about it – maybe often – without ever understanding anything. It's the peril concealed on every page of a book. You think you know. And yet.

You need to have lived. Otherwise you don't see things. You imagine them. You create them. For a long time I created the world before I came to it, from the books in Papa's library.

You don't experience things as they really are. When you recognize that, the world becomes a different place. It's no longer a habit, the sum of all your accumulated certainties: it becomes a question. A hesitation. When I say I'm a human being, it's a question.

Some things are certain: humans are mammals, just like the whales in the river, the hares on the island nearby, the mare and Onile's dog, the goat in the shed that gives milk from the teats on her belly, that gives milk to drink, like the milk from the mainland cows that we use to make curds.

Other certainties, learned from books: that humans suckle their offspring at the breast, have a heart with four chambers, a nervous system, a warm body, and hair. But not feathers. Humans aren't birds. They can't fly.

My mother was a bird. In her own mind, especially. Then in the fresh sea air, with her arms outstretched, spinning. She was an Arctic tern uttering piercing cries. With so many journeys in her mind. Always ready to dive beak-first. To cleave the air. To plummet.

Inside my head, my mother was a bird. Fragile. Aggressive, but frail.

Here's the quandary: my mother was a human, but a bird as well. And as far as I remember as a child, she never fed me at her breast. I'm a human being too: I look like the pictures you see in books. Don't I?

Onile, who always has an answer to my questions, tells me that of course I'm a human being, that we both are. And then he returns to his black notebook. With a little half-smile. That little smile of his.

What I understand from that is that all humans aren't equal. There are some who can feed and some who can be fed. There are some who can't feed, and some who can't be fed. Some live on islands. Others in towns. I imagine cities full of humans feeding at the breast. There's milk in the children's mouths, it pours over the sidewalks. It's beautiful. A milky scene.

But then I can't really understand what makes you human. It's not your body, nor talking that comes of its own accord, nor twisted ideas, nor morals too strict for anyone to stick to. It's not the constant breathing, the hair blown in the wind, the gazing into water, the dreams, the fear, the love. Being human is what people do all over the world. Not on an island in the river. Not on some foggy archipelago. Being human means to be something that teems everywhere. In a city, with people, people, and more people, always on the move, running (often), walking (rarely), eating, talking to themselves, with cockeyed notions, never caring a hoot about morals, driving, riding bikes, tripping up, cursing, touching one another, my God do they touch one another, brushing against one another, clinging to one another. With people who don't have a tree to hug so they hug on street corners, who are in love, like those two guys that fascinate me so, kissing each other on the mouth with their heads a little bent, like lovers, as if they were lovers. People everywhere, in every shape and form, with all kinds of appearances and in all sorts of colours, Baudelaire's poems were right, in all sorts of colours.

Beings. Human beings.

I'm a human being. That's what came out of my mouth when I arrived in Montreal. Right after they came to get me. After they found me, alone, exhausted, sitting on the shore in the chilly shade of the cliff.

When I heard Montreal was an island, I said: Yes. I shouted (nearly): Yes! I'd wanted an island. Well, another island. They told me it was an island, a city. So I thought of water all around me, a sufficient, steady wind, and at the same time a city, a real city. With milk in the children's mouths. But it was a mainland. With people. People everywhere. Humans. An endless flood of congregating beings.

Later, I'd have my memory of that shock. On Place des Arts, naked among everyone, like hundreds of men and women taking directions from a photographer. Finally understanding that I'm a human. What that means. That I'm a body in the crowd. A naked human. At the same time a part and a whole. The human I hadn't been until I came to the mainland.

You're not a human when you live on your island, alone. Not even when you're naked.

I'm Dorothée paying her third visit to Rose Brouillard. There's also a resurgence, and a failure, of memory.

This is the third time that I've come and that she looks surprised, as if she's trying to place me somewhere in her head. For the third time, introducing myself doesn't help, she doesn't remember a thing. Until I rebaptize myself as Dorothée, like she wants. I'm Dorothée. She calls me her cat, the African girl, and asks me how Baudelaire is doing, if he has looked after me properly, if he's still as much in love, and then she tries to take my hands and turn them over, for she wants to see my pink palms and burst out laughing, like a child.

Your hands are pink inside, she tells me. Your hands are like mouths, like mouths at the end of each arm, pink inside, with nails instead of teeth.

And I'm Rose, just Rose, she always says. Don't put me into a fog.

Then I feel discouraged, for she doesn't remember anything about yesterday, nor the day before. She doesn't remember me, but does remember this Dorothée I seem to remind her of. Nor does she remember my camera or the questions I asked. Yet I'd like to believe her when she does remember something: all those days working in the factory since she moved to the city, the way there and home again, the sewing machines, all those sewing machines, the sound of hers as it responds to the pressure of her foot on the pedal, the rise and fall of her foot, the sound of the other machines encouraging one another, that uneven thrumming that continued day and night, you'd almost think, from when she arrived in the city till the factory closed. I want to believe her when she talks about days of yore without batting an eyelid, about the fishing, the drying, the salting, and the smell. And about tarping for winter, setting snares on the island opposite, skinning the hares caught on the island opposite, that smell again, that smell of skinned hares, that same reek. About the long walks across the ice, the seal hunt, and fishing in winter through a hole in the ice. Her father's solitary drinking bouts, his drinking songs, her mother's tears and lamentations, all those details, and the squabbles.

I'm Onile confronting his solitude, which he's reluctant to admit. And then singing on a boat in the middle of the river, a tune no one knows.

Singing by himself, on the stir of the river.

> *Laurent, Laurent's leaving,*
> *Timdelam, timdelidelam*
> *Laurent, Laurent's leaving,*
> *But I'll find another*
>
> *But I'll find another*
> *But I'll find another*
> *There in the village,*
> *There in the village,*
> *Timdelam, timdelidelam*
>
> *There in the village,*
> *There in the village,*
> *A young one, and smart*
> *To be my apprentice,*
>
> *Laurent, Laurent's leaving,*
> *Timdelam, timdelidelam*
> *Laurent, Laurent's leaving,*
> *But I'll find another*

Fortunately there's a wind on the river. Fortunately it dries cheeks, dries tears on cheeks. Then it dries the snot under your nose, when you've taken care to wipe your moustache on your shirt elbow. Fortunately there's a wind.

> *Timdelam, timdelidelam*
> *On the river,*
> *On the St. Lawrence.*

Laurent. Three years already, but it seems like forever. A lively lad, a young village lad lent me for the work. Sharing my hopes, my space, my food, the household chores, the work, the dense smell of fish that envelops you. The silence too. Laurent. A true lad of his time. Coming in through the open door like a sharp blast of wind, before it slams behind him. Warning: the Germans have come this far. They've been spotted to the east, and in the Gaspé. Cursing the Germans, the fascists, our enemies.

Laurent, a sudden blast. That's how he'll have passed through my life. Before setting off to die over there.

Luckily, there was the wind.

In my life, his enthusiasm, hard to keep up with, so strong because ... why? Because he's young, of course, and so strong because he has joined up, of course. He's leaving, he wants to fight. When others of his age would rather hide away on the island and be forgotten, when no French Canadians are willing to let their sons enlist, he, my Laurent, so precious to me, who I need, this near-son of mine, has chosen to set off for the lands where they're fighting. He'd rather go and make war where it's happening. He has accepted the consequences.

It's 1942. We'll never forget. Laurent leaving his river behind, and me as well. Leaving the whole island behind. And the other islands. And everything I'd have left to him, if he'd stayed. His country. His future.

Waste no time. Go to the village. Never mind the sky lowering over the estuary. I'm not afraid of the sea. It's the mainland that makes my head spin.

Waste no time. Go to the village. Find a helper, to replace my helper – a second Laurent.

Another blast of wind. A lasting one.

A replacement. A second Laurent. One who can read and write. Count and work. One who can bear the solitude, one who's already alone, someone trustworthy, not too talkative. One who can bear life's hardships. A Laurent who can understand that the river will outlive every war. And nothing else matters.

I'm Vigneault the sacristan, appearing unexpectedly. He's in his apartment on rue Racine. In front of him a glass of gin, and a second one that he'll drink with an improbable floral chorus.

It's empty, my apartment, empty. Even more than usual since she came, that little black girl looking for Rose Brouyar. I can't stand the yammering of the TV; I've left its raucous monologue to be stifled in the silence of the living room.

On the table in front of me, a stubby glass with a wide bottom into which I regularly pour the next shot of gin. It must be for an hour now that the glass has been dropping back empty onto the wooden table. I have all those stories inside my head, haunting, tormenting me. That vague memory knocking about in the rear of my skull: Keeper Onile entering the shop. Onile in the shop in Sainte-Marie; the sudden silence, and all the other villagers' eyes turned on him.

My cousins have come back to the kitchen. There's nothing unusual in that, for when it happened they'd come to the shop with their mother. So my cousins have returned to the kitchen, around me. Another glass of gin and we'll imagine it together: it was Keeper Onile, remember? In the store in Sainte-Marie, coming in, removing his headgear, and holding it as if at half-mast. My gossipy cousins remember it, for they were there.

I'm Vigneault the sacristan, pouring himself another glass of gin, to keep up appearances.

They were young, with their plaits and white dresses, each with a big bow at the waist, and each with her own colour, even the twins.

Around us, the others, older, grown-ups. Their surprise, their reaction, their comments. These others are: old Chevillard, who's just lost his barn in a fire; he's with his son, the delicate one, who was the sacristan back then, I didn't think much of him; there's Madame So-and-So and also Marie-Someone-Else, some of those women with a gaggle of young ones, all there for the groceries, what they need for cooking, and for cloth to sew – the sorts of things you can get from only one place – from the Bourgeois in the village.

Well, if it isn't the hermit paying a call. So many reactions: chuckles, sighs, and murmurs, but mostly a lot of murmurs, the frayed edge of a wave on the beach. There was Onile with his floppy beret in one fist, clutched over his heart. That's how he was, Onile.

Respect. A man should stand like that to show respect. Some were better at it than others. My father too, I'd seen him do the same, mostly in church, but less elegantly than Onile in company. Those he didn't encounter very often deserved to see his head.

He was welcomed like a man of strength, the poor devil – that's what they call him sometimes, "the poor devil," depending on what they've got to say about him. He's welcomed like a man of strength, but the poor devil shrivels up as the inquisitive ones, the ones who've seen his dinghy tied up at the dock, enter the store to hear what he has to say. When there was a crowd, old Bourgeois would keep an eye on his stock like a jealous lover on his girlfriend. He suspected his son of dipping his hand in the jar as soon as his back was turned.

Then: Onile rooted in the doorway, struggling to emerge from his island silence, beret clutched to his heart, his mouth half-open.

I'm the spectral spinsters beginning to talk like the villagers of former days, while Vigneault the sacristan pours another shot of gin into his empty glass.

He's changed, did you notice?
He's getting old, you'd hardly know him.
Are you sure it's really him?

The Keeper, isn't it?

Or maybe the saver of souls. It was him found poor Uncle Robert for us after his net tried to give him to the sea.

The last time he came . . . it must be a good year ago?

It's him, do you realize? He saved Gervais, Rodrigue's boy from up above, two years past. That family'd be decimated but for him.

Dry-bones Onile?

Hidden away like that on his island, he must be into smuggling, for sure!

You'd expect him to be bigger, yet he's no more solid than Papa. For someone who breaks up the ice, he's a bit skinny.

I'm Vigneault the sacristan, finding it quite comic listening to his cousins, whom in fact he hasn't seen for years.

When you're face to face with a legend, you seldom realize it. But one thing was sure in the Bourgeois's store that day, Brouillard only had to open his mouth for everyone to pay attention.

I'm a man and three women declaiming solemnly, like a chorus, while poor Onile is rooted in the doorway of the general store:

My apprentice, Laurent, he wants to go off to the war.

I'm Vigneault the sacristan, taking on the air of a storyteller with no audience in a no longer recognizable apartment.

It falls like a cold shower on the assembly, a deluge like those downpours on the river that come down on you in a curtain; it's a surprise, a shock. The dumbfounded audience understands the situation; even we youngsters have grasped it.

Like everywhere in Quebec, the people in the village of Sainte-Marie had said no to conscription in Mackenzie King's referendum. They'd fought hard to protect their progeny when the government representatives first visited the village to sound people out: If you want cannon fodder, then start by building us a road! For so long the village has been cut off, accessible only by boat, for the road skirts the plateau that rises up north of the village.

They understand why the Keeper has come. They know he loved Laurent like his own son, and that he'll be hard to replace. Not because he was such a great worker, but because on the island the solitude can become unbearable. Long weeks of silence, seeing only your own face in the mirror and Onile's with its moustache, hungover Onile, dry-bones Onile. That's what they called him in the village too.

With a little gin in the bottom of the glass, facing me, Flore starts to laugh, remembering the answer that issued from the silence of the subdued assembly: Maybe it's time you took a wife, Keeper Onile!

General laughter inside the store. Then another voice added: Bring the priest and we'll marry Brouillard.

Even Onile laughed, a sign that everyone had found the situation amusing. Everyone, that is, except two men at the counter who didn't even smile. The one who had offered that valuable advice. And old Chevillard, who knew what was in the speaker's mind.

The one who had spoken finally turned to the man from off the sea. I felt like a child clinging to my father's sleeve. Onile's moustache settled back over his set lips like a heron treading foot in marshy ground. No more likelihood of a smile on that face.

The silence had to fall again completely for the man who had first uttered the jest to come out with it: I've got just the girl for you. A good-looking one, with strong shoulders, well used to hard work, in the fields, in the cowshed, to doing everything in the house, bread, pies, soup. She's just a bit hare-brained, for she's still young. The island'll soon cure her of that.

Between my spectral cousins and myself, a litre of gin, straight off. The white heart affixed to the bottle of De Kuyper hasn't sat below the level of the nectar for a while now. Another glass, bottoms up. It's good for the tubes, gin. I'm coughing less. Much less.

Maybe I'm forgetting what I'm doing.

Among the four of us, in the kitchen – and Onile too, shaking off his shirt. And his headgear that he tucks under one arm. Onile rubbing his palms, each thumb gripped in the opposite hand, a quirk of his when making a serious decision.

Think it over, said the father of the proffered bride. Think it over well. She could help you on the island. Liven up your winters. You never know, she might give you a little one of your own. A child of your own, to go to sea in your place. The war will be long over before he grows up.

It was a powerful argument: a woman for a helper. For entertainment. And a son to grow up.

All right. Let the woman come.

In the kitchen, after a giggle, the cousins form a procession, chanting psalms. There's an echo in the empty apartment, which becomes a church, the church at Sainte-Marie. I'm a choirboy behind the altar, rosy cheeked, hair slicked down. And in front of the priest, the other choirboys, and me, Onile and his moustache, craggy Onile, dry-bones Onile, Onile who's double the age of the woman on his arm, an erect young woman, her face expressionless. Just once, a pinch of the lips. That was when the priest blessed the union. I was the only one noticed it, that pinch of the lips.

To the humming of the three flowers, I fall asleep on the table.

I'm Onile in his bedroom; he's not alone; he's with the girl plucked from the coast, and it's a first time.

My house. My new wife and me. Soon, skin against skin. New blood on the island. Warm blood, yes. A woman to help. And to be lovely in this place.

She'll be lovely in the smell of the food cooking all day long. Lovely when her dress bothers her, hitched up to her thigh when she's milking the goat, cutting and washing the vegetables, or feeding hay or meal to the mare.

She'll be lovely on anxious nights, when she'll stay asleep, keeping the bed warm while I go out on the headland to make sure no one has struck the reef.

She'll be lovely getting up to care for the son that will have slithered from her body. I'll never be fully asleep with her between my sheets:

I'll watch her emerge from the bed, her wraithlike figure floating out of the room, her figure returning, so softly, to slip back beside me, like lard melting into the hollow of my spoon. She'll be lovely despite her sadness, despite her anger at being plucked from the coast. Lovely in spite of it all. She'll be the light of a keeper with no light.

She's already lovely to see around. Lovely in my bedroom, not giving me a glance. She's lovely even if her body keeps its distance, on the defensive, huddled to the wall, on the far side of the bed.

She undressed as if performing a duty, with the deliberate gestures of one willing enough, yet impatient to have it over and done with. Her full body, her rounded belly, her chapped hands, her bush, dense like an unkempt beard, her straight back, her erect head. She doesn't cave in easily.

I'd never seen a woman naked before. Never for real. So that's what it's like.

It's a lovely thing.

I'm the new mistress of Onile's house, the mistress of the island, standing in the bedroom, rocking like a buoy.

What are you waiting for? You wanted a little wife, and now you've got one. It's time to take her. So take her.

I'm Onile before the body of his new fury of a wife, the one plucked from the coast, his downfall. Around them, the backdrop to this unique spectacle.

I can hear: her anger, the creaking of the planks as they resist the wind, the apprentice's steps on the veranda. He'll stay on two weeks more, Laurent, to help the new arrival. To help my wife.

My wife. It feels strange to say that.

To show her what her work will be. In the meantime he goes about the most urgent tasks himself. Leaving the newlyweds in their bedroom. To rest for a few hours before nightfall.

She enfolds her heavy bosom with her crossed arms, covering as best she can the large brown nipple crowning each breast.

Not like that, please. Not like that, I say, to reassure her. When I speak, my moustache tickles right down to my lower lip. I should have trimmed it.

I was trying to reassure her, but I frightened her instead: a glimmer of fear shone in her liquid, agate eyes. She begins to weep. Her body goes limp, turning into a huge mollusc in the bedroom, mollusc pink, mollusc skin, swimming in its sea juices, in its tears and mucus, with a malevolent glance, sharp as a pointed blade.

Grasp her under the armpits. Help her to her feet. Then to walk to the bed. Then to sit down on it, gently. For that's how I imagine a woman should behave. Then to stretch out, on her left side. On the bed, the two heavy, fleshy sacs of her breasts, which a moment ago hung towards the ground, lie flat under her folded arm.

Spread a fresh sheet over her coiled body, a white cotton one that clings to her. Go round the bed, finish undressing, quickly, since I must, and slip under the same sheet, and simply hold her against me.

I feel the skin of another body against mine. It's the first time since I left my mother's arms. That was, shall we say, a long time ago. Such softness. Such warmth. They might have been enough.

She calms down. She is only half-weeping, her body still racked by spasms of sadness, anger, and bitterness. It's a reaction I'm powerless to resist, that affects my flesh.

Her young bride's eyes are closed. She continues to grow calm. Soon, her body will convulse with spasms, not of distress but of desire. For desire will always have its way. She'll allow her new husband to penetrate her. Without my moustache that tickles her neck, cheek, and shoulder when I kiss them, I could be anyone.

I'm Laurent, waging war in his mind, soon just waging war, soon, very soon.

It must be two years now that they've been here, going up and down, and I've been telling myself they should have swallowed me up and taken me with them. For two years the two Royal Navy patrol boats have been plowing their furrow of white foam along the strategic part of the river, between Gaspé and Saint-Jean-de-l'Île d'Orléans. For the enemy might be there too, or so people say: he might well be there too.

For two years they've been going up and down, wrenching me a little more from the island each time. When they appear, Onile flies into a rage:

> come down to earth, Laurent,
> you're a fisherman, Laurent,
> harness yourself to the net, gut the fish, dry the
>   fish, you're a fisherman,
> those fine boats that set you dreaming, they could
>   very well kill you,
> those boats in your dreams are fighting a war, not
>   just tracing those white furrows you wonder
>   at, so neat and clean,
> you're a fisherman, Laurent, my Laurent,
> you've already chosen your side.

He doesn't understand that that's exactly the side I want to defend, to protect. It's the side of the fishermen, their wives, their descendants.

Onile wages war on storms. I'll wage mine against armies. From here I can hear their boots crushing children's skulls, see their gloved hands violating girls; I hear their weapons and their threats from beyond the river, from beyond the estuary, from across the ocean; their weapons and their threats that take advantage of the winter and ice to send chills down my spine. Tomorrow it will be our children, our Étiennettes, our Rose-Aimées, our Jean-Marcs, our Andrés. Tomorrow it will be our girls' turn to be pawed and raped. Then will be a time for angry tears, with no army worth a damn, with only our anger to avenge them and drive out the enemy with a few hefty kicks to the behind. Or guns loaded with rock salt. Unarmed, we'll just have to watch them descend on us and smash us.

They sent a letter. To all the lighthouses along the river. And even though Onile isn't really a lightkeeper, even though he's only considered one by those who know his story, he was sent a copy.

Like every time a letter comes, Onile opened it in front of me. That's how he taught me to read – just a little, enough to get along. All those words that take time to decipher.

Monsieur Onile Brouillard,

I can read that because I recognize those three words, *Monsieur* and *Onile* and *Brouillard*. I can recognize them for they're always there in the same place on the page when he unfolds it. He reads me the message, and points to each word as it comes from his mouth.

Onile Brouillard wasn't really a lightkeeper, he had neither the light, nor the pay, nor the duties. But everyone from Gaspé to Quebec City with an interest in maritime affairs knew him by reputation. He was the man who rises with the wind, who breaks the sheet ice, dry-bones Onile even in a rainstorm, they say, with a laugh, Onile who keeps a lookout, Onile with no lighthouse to keep, but above all Onile who saves lost souls, who brings bodies ashore, when it's not fishermen with open eyes.

He has saved men, Keeper Onile, for he knows the hazards on the river bottom off his lonely headland, the river bottom that tries to drag them all down. Everyone knows what battles he's fought, which ones he's lost and which ones he's won. He's respected wherever there's a lighthouse on the river and estuary. Respected for who he is as much as for the lives he's saved. The other keepers treat him like one of their own, in a way.

When the letter arrived at the Brandy Pot light, where as a younger man Onile had once been employed as the keeper's assistant, they copied it out in an ungainly hand and forwarded it to him. A letter of his own, a copy of the official one. It ordered him to watch out for the slightest cause for concern. For the enemy could be right there, under his very eyes, in our river waters.

In our river. The enemy.

The navy launches that have been patrolling all this time were hunting for Germans. In our river. The enemy. Plotting an attack, whispering inside the muffled resonance of his U-boat. Attempting to blockade. Able to torpedo. Able to come ashore and set fire to everything. To leave the islands as scorched earth. The mainland too.

Onile didn't want to make much of it. His only reaction was to purse his lips and stop reading aloud. Of course he'll keep an eye out. Just like whenever he turns to gaze at the river he watches for all the other possible dangers. But for him the threat isn't real: if the Nazis are just rapists and child killers they'll have no cause to come sneaking up our river. They'll find plenty to keep them occupied without crossing the ocean. As for the Germans, he refuses to believe they're as wicked as they say. He always gives me the example of the one who doesn't come anymore, but who came for six years and even made him the present of that old woodcarver's box he's so proud of. Onile had saved him, that German. Saved him from the river bottom when it tried to drag him under. He helped a German. So, the war, you understand . . .

I think the war will reach even this far. The Germans once tried to buy Anticosti, or at least so the villagers said. They'll come back, and they'll march up our river, like in the rest of the world. They'll dig trenches and set ambushes. This river's well worth the trouble, with so many ships sailing up it, laden with cargo from all parts.

I couldn't live on our island anymore knowing our freedom was defiled. The war will reach to here. The St. Lawrence will run with blood. But when the Germans come, their tears will add salt to the estuary.

The war is here already. At sunrise, I hate the Nazis. I hate them at mealtimes. I curse them in the roar of the waves when the tide is in. Whenever I haul the nets onto the boat, I'm taking up arms against them. You always wage war in your head before you pick up a weapon.

I'm the child Rose before her sinking mother, her singing mother, the essence of sadness, *maluron, lurette*.

I know war waged inside the head. It's grounded in rampant despondency, in Mama's untimely sadness. When she sings songs about war and about swallows:

> *Tell me what's amiss, Françoise,*
> *élongué*
> *Tell me what's amiss, Françoise,*
> *Why are you weeping so?*
> *maluron, lurette*
> *Why are you weeping so?*
> *maluron, luré*

Mama weeping like a forsaken Françoise. Baking bread, or a pie. Cooking a hare. Doing the washing. Hanging out the sheets in a strong wind. Weeping as she sings:

> *But when he was at sea*
> *élongué*
> *But when he was at sea*

Sluicing down the floor. Giving me my bath, scrubbing my back and armpits, cleaning out my ears, brushing my hair. Rubbing me all over as if I was dirty, an incorrigible child, a filthy little thing. As if I was a speck of dirt.

> *I heard the sad bell toll*
> *maluron, lurette*

Another meltdown, it's pouring through every orifice of her face as she chokes on the thought of her soldier dying. Maybe no one could have heard the last lines, which would have had to be read from her lips:

> *I heard the sad bell toll*
> *maluron, luré*

A fit of viscous coughing, with mucus on Mama's lip. She abandons the basket and the white sheets that will never dry there. And the good-smelling food. And her daughter soaking in a basin of dirty water.

Mama giving up.

**I'm the teenage Rose, armed to the teeth. There are blue
clouds, like the smoke of the Cuban revolution.**

I know the kind of war you fight with a finger on the trigger.
I know how to hold a gun.

I'm not too young to have gone to war. But I've done even better:
a revolution.

I'm sixteen. A revolutionary, like those Cuban men. I was fascinated to learn from Papa's newspapers that on an island like Cuba
you can be ready to take up arms to change the course of history.
What can you want to change on an island? Not everything was
explained in the papa-in-the-story's newspapers.

I've no Che or Fidel to follow, but I do have a weapon handy.
Onile keeps it in the living room, over the wardrobe. A gun hung
up like a trophy. You have to be able to protect yourself. Anyone
could come and steal our supplies. Shoot the hares on the nearby
island. Steal all the fruit. Stave in the boat. Leave us on our cliff to
die of hunger.

I've got a weapon. And an implacable master to defeat. One who
controls, leads, and infuriates. Who issues his orders in few words.
Who makes the world the way it is.

At sixteen I've got breasts, energy, desires, and a will of my own.
I'll deal with all that. My headland's an island, and my island is Cuba.
My uprising is a cliff. And the sea bottom is strewn with the seeds of
exotic fruit eaten by bathers. There are kids all around, naked little
boys, brown-skinned, curly-haired kids without any willies because
I don't know anything about that, their bare bottoms in the sea and
sand caught in their bums. And Spanish speakers too. And Russian
speakers who say *shka* at every word and tucked under their arms
they have satellites from the junk shops that I imagine spilling out
from Moscow basements. With their pockets full of rockets – useless
rockets, red ones with white squares like those of Professor Calculus
in Papa's comic book, pasteboard rockets ready to crash in their
anemic flight and burst into flames.

Then I sing:

Neeaykateei keeneea berniay katoyshka!
Layee-layee-layee-layee
layee-layee-layee-layee
layee-layee-layee-layee
Hey!

Or something like that.

I planted signs around the headland, written in a kind of Cyrillic alphabet – actually I use capital letters, turning every second one back to front and adding accents to the consonants.

Most of my signs are written in German. *Mein Zuhause. Mein Insel. Das Meer* – my home, my island, the sea. In Papa's library, as well as the Belgian comic books and all the novels and history books brought by the delivery boy, there's a French-German dictionary.

It's for the ones who'll come back, or so he says. I've never seen a German come ashore here. But apparently it's happened.

Mein Zuhause, my home – there, on the low cliff, the only house that exists, the only one in the whole world.

Mein Insel, it's all around. But *mein Insel* is Cuba too – no matter that I write in German. And even if the water is freezing, even if the beach is grey and stony, even if the waves aren't inviting, even if I wear a head scarf on account of the wind, my island is Cuba, a German Cuba afloat in *das Meer*.

Mein Insel is Cuba. And I'm ready to fight. *Mein Kampf*. It's in the dictionary. I've folded over a corner of the page.

I'm a girl soldier, dressed in green, ready to suffer, ready to shed every drop of my blood for the revolution if necessary, ready to smoke cigars too, since that's a requirement. I roll a few leaves of the sage that's been growing in the garden since my mother's day, put them to dry in the shed along with the firewood, and imitate the pictures in the papa-in-the-story's newspapers that show those bearded Cubans smoking the tropical forest. I smoke up on the cliff with Fidel and a group of other nonchalant revolutionaries, who are searching my list for other wars to fight.

We blow out like this: *ffff*.

Blue clouds: *ffff*.

Blue clouds of sage smoke through the larch trees.

I tell them I don't need them. That it's going to be my fight. *Mein Kampf.*

It's my home. *Mein Zuhause.*

It's my headland.

It's *my* island, mine.

I belong to the sea. To no one else. And I'm ready to start a revolution. Even all by myself, without any bearded cigar smokers.

I've planted my German signs, yelling as loud as I could, yelling the way I imagined it: *mein Zuhause, mein Insel, mein Meer! Mein Kampf!* Then I climbed up on the rock, gun in hand. There, a wind stopped me from falling.

From here, I'll take Papa by surprise. My heart is racing. My head scarf is a nuisance, I'm hot, in spite of the damp wind that's holding me up. It won't hold me up forever. Soon it won't hold me at all. When I put a bullet through him, it will let me drop too.

Nor will Onile, the papa in the story, be able to hold me forever. His face is still calm. He often takes off his floppy hat like that when he wants to mop his brow and the back of his neck with the beret's inside. It's one of the gestures I've seen him make most often. When he's doing the housework. Painting. Repairing the dock, the veranda, the railing. Toiling away. Turning the soil in the garden. Whenever he's hot. He takes off his beret and uses it like a towel to wipe the moist skin of his neck and his high forehead. This time, he does nothing of the sort. He just takes off his floppy beret and that's that. Even though he's hot. He's come running from the house to where I am. Telling himself: She's hiding. Telling himself: She knows the island better than I do.

I'm Onile running, rushing down, out of breath, in a panic, worried. There are his boots, too loose at the ankle, hurting his feet. In his mind the same words turn over ceaselessly, in time with his strides.

She knows the island better than me.

Even when she was four she knew the island better than me. She knows the island better than anyone.

I'm the teenage Rose, no longer able to back down.

He came running. From the house to me. From the living room to the door, from the door to the steps, from the steps to the dock, and I heard: Daughter! He has run from the dock to the beach and from there to the tall cliff, up the other side. As if he knew that was where he'd find me. That's what he was hoping. He's in a sweat.

I'm scared. I'm sixteen and I'm scared. I'm sixteen, I've got breasts, energy, and desires, and I'm headstrong, but I'm scared. The way you're scared when you're face to face with yourself.

Who doesn't desire his father's death?

That's in a book by a Russian. Dostoevsky. In Onile's library there's *The Brothers Karamazov*. I've read it. So has Papa.

Who doesn't desire his father's death?

I'm scared because there's a gun in the situation, between my body and his. I have the butt and the trigger at my end. All that's left for him is to be the target. Even if he moved, even if he tried to join me. He'd still be the target, for the one and only reason that he's at the wrong end of the gun.

That way he has of looking at me. With such love. Even when I have him in my sights.

In a revolution you either win or die. I couldn't die, so I had to win. Papa knew that. He raised a white flag: his hand in front of him, level with his face, motioning to me to wait, declaring his readiness to talk.

You're already the mistress around here. What more do you want? He asked.

Louder: What is it you want?

I don't like it when he takes that tone. That out-of-control voice. When it gets away from him. Him, always so calm. I can see Fidel beside me, a cigar gripped in the crook of his index finger, his hair cut short, his unkempt beard. He proclaims, in such a way that Onile can't hear: We want neither bread without liberty, nor liberty without bread. And me, who already had liberty and bread, what more did I want? Good question.

I could have said I wanted the mainland. I could have said the village. I could have said the city. But there's so much to ask for. When you turn towards the mainland you hear the same roar of rolling breakers, that thunder of every moment, but with no lightning to illuminate the landscape. I could have said I wanted the coast. But I said it was music I wanted. The radio had disappeared at the same time as Mama. I'd missed it.

Papa had two kinds of anger. There was the kind he'd indulge in unrestrainedly because there was no one around to hear. When he struck a stone with the pickaxe and felt the pain surge through his whole body. When the village delivery boy made a mistake in the order and brought too much flour or too little, too many potatoes or too few, too much scotch or not enough. When a boat ventured too close to the treacherous reefs and risked running aground. Those were his noisiest outbursts, but not the most terrible.

His worst rages were the ones he suffered in silence. Because they were steeped in disappointment. And there's no consolation for disappointment.

Except maybe music.

I'm Onile on the page of an exercise book. A few handwritten sentences, as if in italics – ink-strokes shaped on the lined page by painstaking fingers:

How could she! I should have been beside myself in one of the worst fits of anger in my life, I was in the sights of my own gun, yet nothing happened. I was stunned, and moved. I've loved that child more than anything.

I'll lose my soul for that daughter of mine. Like her mother. And like with her mother I couldn't help it. I just felt the urge to take her in my arms. I think that's the sort of thing a mother should do.

When I go to the village I'll inquire about a gramophone. Maybe Bourgeois will know where to find one of those old things. If I hadn't smashed the radio, this would never have happened. She has won. Her revolution will have succeeded. She'll have her music. Not just the roar of the breakers, not just the wind and the storms, not just the rustle of leaves. Real music.

But all the same, something struck me from the barrel of that gun.

I'm Dorothée inside the Pontiac with Rose beside her. At 110 kilometres an hour everything vibrates and flies past.

Shaky images, with the camera resting on the dash. It falls. It was a bird picking at some dead thing in the centre of the road. We hit it. I've lost Rose's image, but not her voice.

I'm Rose reciting a few odd lines of poetry, taken from a banned collection that occupied a few hours of her youth.

Jolted pictures, the camera sliding on the dashboard is directed at the road instead of Rose. The corpse of a bird on the asphalt.

> *The sun beat down upon that rot*
> *As if to roast it through*
> *Rend'ring great Nature a hundredfold*
> *What she had joined as one*

I'm Dorothée in the car, with Rose beside her. The same speed, with everything still sliding and slipping past. Before the eyes and in the mind.

I asked her permission to film her during the trip. The camera sits on the dash or on the armrest between us, taking her from a low angle. We talk, we fall silent. Usually, she looks straight ahead, never smiling, concentrating, never looking in my direction, as if nothing existed but a scrap of skyline.

Also, the fields that mean something to her. And the river, towards which she dare not glance. Whenever I turn my head her eyes are lowered, or she's staring at the road or the sky, or is looking at the dash, reaching out, as if to check with her fingertips that it's really there in front of her. She's beautiful against the fleeting landscape alongside the highway. For a long time now her old body has been a missile, a foreign body in the blinding light. It's travelling too fast through space and time to check itself. That's what it is, the memory she lacks. Nothing clings to her.

Regularly, her fingers move to the back of her neck. She would do that already the first times I met her in her apartment, but the film from the car shows how tense and more frequent the gesture is. Her bony hand raised to massage her nape with the sound of flesh rubbing on flesh, a quick *tsh, tsh, tsh*, rolling a few hairs into a matted coil. Then the hand falling back on her thigh, weary from the journey, giving it a perfunctory rub: it's her poor circulation. And then that glance, always the same, like a look of surprise.

She asks: Where are we going?

That bleating voice. I'm not in the picture, but you can hear my answer clearly: Home, Madame Brouillard. To your old home. To where you were born.

Later, she asks again, in the same voice: Where are we going?

I can be heard repeating to her, with all the patience in the world: To your old home, Madame Brouillard, to the house on the headland.

And again.

To your old home, Madame Brouillard, to the Keeper's headland.

To your old home Madame Brouillard. You know, where the river and the skyline will recognize you.

I could have told her anything. The stress had finally gotten her lost along the road from Montreal to Sainte-Marée. When your name is Rose Brouillard, being out of your element is only a figure of speech; leaving home means going out the window. It's recognizing how many truths that liar of a window can tell.

I could have told her anything. Her cracked old mind, lost along the way, would have accepted it. Realizing this, I wondered if the whole thing was such a good idea. Bringing her to Sainte-Marée and taking her across the water, back to the Keeper's house. Photographing her, capturing it all on video because tourists really like to see people and places. Before I could discuss it with Rose, I'd said yes right away to the guy at Plumules Nord who explained the project to me, for I'd really wanted to do this for her – to allow her to break through the city's walls and rediscover the wide horizon, its gusting winds, its sweet air, and all that's happening there.

The picture jumps: the camera has slipped again. It must have been upset by one of the lazy curves in the highway or by an unexpected slope. Catching it just in time to stop it falling, I make a sudden swerve that leaves us shaken. Then you glimpse the untidy car, the bare skin of my arm, almost my face, my expression – of relief, obviously, at having avoided the worst. Then the windshield with its reflections and the dirt sticking to it, and that swollen landscape slipping away.

At that moment, camera in hand, I took the opportunity to film a few shots through the driver-side window of the river and the rounded hills of the South Shore. It's not a good idea to use the camera while you're driving: most of what you get is blurred and shaky, unusable. But to preserve the memory, that's another thing.

I replaced the camera on the curved surface of the glowing dash with its texture like aged skin, darker than mine, and then you see the windshield again, the passenger-side window, the old woman's face badly framed, always with the same expression, her mouth sealed by the same absence of a smile, by the same mute inquiry: Where are we going? she asks.

Home, Madame Brouillard. To Keeper Onile's house.

I'm a tourist who has been able to convince her flyfisher husband to go on a trip. Also, the arguments she found.

It's been a long drive from home, that's for sure. With my feet on the dash I stretch the back of my thighs and massage my kneecaps. I can understand how he's finding it long, with his foot on the gas for nearly five hours now. In spite of all the stops I let him make.

He grumbles. Sighs. Plays with the knob on the radio, changing the station every few minutes, unable to find anything worth listening to. He'll never find anything decent anyway. But he keeps on. It fills the time. And the silence.

He's here, no question. He came with me. But I need more than that: I need him to believe in the idea, to share some of my enthusiasm. To find somewhere deep inside an echo of my desire to go on this trip with him. We've been to Europe, the United States, Brazil. People should take time to appreciate what we've got at home too. I think that goes without saying.

He wants us to stop, anywhere, at the next interchange, at the first hotel. He wants us to call it a day, to stop and shut ourselves up in some bedroom, period. Except that when we got there he'd keep on like before. He'd carry on with the TV like he does with the radio, channel surfing till he fell asleep, and then sulk at me the next morning. He'd end by turning his back to me in our chance bed.

No, no. Only thirty kilometres more, come on!

We're getting there.

He rolls his eyes. He complains about the lightning that's cleaving the eastern sky. Just where we're heading. He sulks.

That splendid mouth of his. He has such nice lips. They make me want to kiss him all the time. Except that his sulking shows I've not won him over yet. He'll need some convincing. Then I explain to him that Sainte-Euphrasie, the village where we're to spend the night, is thirty minutes from the ferry, so if we sleep there we can be on time to board. Even without hurrying. That it won't be too difficult.

Usually the it-won't-be-too-difficult argument works well.

Then I mention the discount (almost as much as the tax). I explain how they keep tourists captive in the region: if you sleep in one of the hotels on the list you get a deal on all the activities during your stay, even in the restaurant. That's good if it helps us save money. I ask him if he thinks it's a good thing.

Aha, he agrees all the same. He's still sulking, but he nods. The economic argument. For when it-won't-be-too-difficult hasn't worked.

He yawns, as if that made the case for what he wants. Me, I just go on massaging. And racking my brain.

I tell him about the river – the Rivière Fourchette, near Sainte-Euphrasie. Though I'm not particularly convinced myself, I say maybe he could go and try a few casts around dawn. He scarcely glances at the brochure, and sighs. That's not going to win him over. Not this time.

I try to make him see that the time we save will allow us to reach the federal dock to catch the first ferry of the day and get to our destination early. That would give us time to visit the old fish-salting works restored in the early nineties and made into a museum.

I open my brochure. It describes the old salting works. The historical artifacts are on the ground floor: the fishing equipment, agricultural machinery, old photographs, old furniture – the lot. I'm losing him. The second floor has been designed for exhibitions, to display the work of local artists – the kind who paint landscapes with autumn leaves and sunsets and daisies in late June. Beautiful work by local artists.

I tried my best to keep a straight face. Really I did. He rolled his eyes and threw me an incredulous glance. I could read: You're not serious, you can't be serious, you're having me on, right? I couldn't help but burst out laughing, and that drew a shadow of a smile from him. So far so good. A hint of complicity.

I bring the brochure up to the steering wheel to show him, waxing enthusiastic: Look, there's even animal paintings. How cute: look, a duck.

He presses his lips together and tells me that's enough, says he can't take it anymore. He's only half-laughing. With one hand on his thigh I try a little harder to convince him, and I tell him about the painting by Marc-Aurèle Fortin, who is supposed to have painted a tree in Sainte-Marée when on holiday in the region. Apparently they've even put a bench on the very spot where he sat to paint.

I suggest to him that after seeing the old salting works we could go on for dinner at La Grave, pointing out that it's a four-star restaurant, offering five four-star courses, and from the terrace at sunset there'll be a special view of Friday's incantation.

He asks about the incantation. That's a positive: he's curious. I explain that it's a performance by the women, in a kind of trance, chilled to the bone as they kneel in the mud along the river's edge, pleading with the sea and the sea gods to protect the fishermen who have gone to sea for the week. It's said to be a local tradition. If the brochure's to be believed, that seems to be our only opportunity to witness the incantation, for it's only performed once a week. So I insist: I want to be there for the incantation.

Then the day after tomorrow it'll be the excursion to Keeper's Island. He's sure to like that. We'll spend the night on an island in that archipelago dotted along the horizon opposite Sainte-Marée.

He throws in the towel. Another yawn, a deeper one, with a dry whistle in his throat. He rubs his forehead with his palm. Since he's started to lose his hair he does that more often.

He asks if I'd like to drive for a while. That's how he puts it, with that malicious expression he always puts on when he knows I've gotten the better of him. A wry little smile and raised eyebrows: Wouldn't you like to drive for a while?

He knows I can't, that I'm blind when I drive at night. That I'm very uneasy with all those headlights sweeping over my face. He knows that; he knows it perfectly well. He knows I can't, since the accident, that I can't drive for a while, as he puts it, at night.

He knows it infuriates me when he throws it in my face. He's trying to be smart. It's my turn to roll my eyes and sigh. He seizes the opportunity to complain. He says he knows. That it's all very well to want to travel until late at night, but that in addition to being expensive, it's tiring.

Well, if he hadn't taken so long to get ready. Yet his bags were packed for him. And then there were all those stops he wanted to make. Here along the river. There in a park. At the restaurant, just before noon. Sitting at that out-of-the-way table. Wanting to read the newspapers, since they were handy. And the rest stops, all those rest stops, to pee the coffee he'd drunk. We'd be there by now without his delays. But I mustn't take the bait. Keep cool. Never give up.

Thirty kilometres, darling. Thirty kilometres to the hotel we've (I've) booked.

I'm Dorothée in the motel, wrapped in clean sheets, in the deep rumble of Rose's sleep. There's also the memory of that sleeping student.

Her old woman's body in the other bed. She's breathing noisily through her mouth, making the soft back of her palate vibrate.

She first fell asleep on the chair brought outside, with her legs, leaden from the journey, stretched out on a wicker ottoman. Over her knees, the madder-coloured woollen rug I found in the trunk of my car. The river overflows from her eyes. For a moment, a teardrop leaves me in doubt: is it emotion, or the wind? Or maybe just a yawn.

When I saw her, head leaned back, lips apart, and eyelids drooping, three-quarters closed, I thought it better not to waken her right away. Sometimes you don't dare disturb someone who's sleeping like that.

At the CEGEP there was this boy, a strange boy, who I often went to see after my classes. A friend, let's say. From his open window we could get onto the flat roof of an annex to the student residence. From there we enjoyed the sun and the amused security of voyeurs sure they are well hidden. If you can see without being seen, you can poke fun without fearing the consequences. The passersby, the banality of their daily lives, their miserable little dramas, always made us giggle. When they heard our sniggers, intruding obscenely into their serious conversations, the people we were watching would freak out, look around, and walk on, noses constantly over one shoulder, walking faster, reduced to silence.

One day in May when I paid him a visit, intending to make use of his improvised terrace, he didn't answer when I knocked.

I was about to turn away, but in the end I went back and tried the doorknob. When I heard the latch click, I stuck my head through the half-open door and saw him lying there stark naked on his bed that he'd pushed beneath the window, bathed in sunlight and glistening with sweat. I remember he wasn't especially handsome: a bit scrawny, as you might expect of an undernourished student, with a lanky frame and a bony chest. It was the situation that made him desirable. He represented a serene, relaxed abandon. No one could see him lying there, except me when I opened the door. Maybe he was expecting me. Like after our nights on the town, when we'd stagger back to his room after the bars closed, clinging to each other and getting into the same bed, finishing inside each other, and wakening with the same embarrassment, overcome by the same silence. I could have gone in, taken him in my hand, into my mouth, said his name, surprised him. But when some people are sleeping like that, you dare not disturb them.

I gazed for a moment until he turned towards me, offering his butt to the unseeing landscape, one leg drawn up close to him on the mattress. The movement startled me. But he was really asleep, or else putting on a convincing show. I shut the door on this picture that I've always kept to myself. I'd liked finding him like that – seeing him asleep, so untroubled.

I enjoyed seeing Rose asleep too. She was lovely, sitting like that, breathing in the river through her open mouth, using it as a sleeping potion.

I left her to restore her energy, imagining she was recharging her batteries with all the things she had missed about the river since she left it. I walked on the dikes and along the shore, stirring up the shingle with a toe, pulling myself up onto the rocks that surfaced parallel to the river, avoiding the brown seaweed, the matted green mosses, and all the slick surfaces on which I might have slipped.

And I enjoyed the sunset.

There aren't any sunsets in Sainte-Marée. The sun just vanishes, sliding down into the woods at the back. It's like that all along the North Shore, in the little villages that cling to the steep coastline. They only know the sun's colours from dawn.

That's how it is on Keeper's Island too, unless you go round it. And even then the sun will be swallowed up by the forest on the mainland long before it sets.

Rose knows all that.

When I got back a storm was rumbling inland, to the east, in contrast with the cloudless sunset over the landscape. Rose had just wakened, I think. As I approached she held out an arm to let me know she wanted me to help her up. It was to go to bed for the night. She complained of the cold: I spread the woollen blankets and my bedspread over her. She shut her eyes and let herself drift off without a word. That's how it goes, as I very well know, when you're used to living in silence.

And now in the semidarkness I stare at her old woman's body in the other bed, her dishevelled hair and her open lips, through which she's breathing loudly. I also hear the quiet snoring through her mouth, and the occasional grunts she makes deep in her throat. Strangely, I find it all very soothing; it reminds me of my grandmother when I used to spend summers with her as a child.

I'm Dorothée, unable to sleep. She's thinking of what comes next.

Tomorrow, Rose in Sainte-Marée.

Tomorrow, filming Rose in Sainte-Marée. Rediscovering. The whole thing.

The day after tomorrow, Rose on the tourist boat to the island. Filming her. And the photographer. I mustn't forget the photographer. For a permanent record. I'll have to take care of that.

Then Rose on the island. Her island. Brouillard Island. Keeper's Island.

I'm that nice neighbour, uneasy going into Rose's empty apartment. There's everything going on inside her head, that stream of words with no periods, commas, or capitals, like when there are people around to hear her.

what i see

the apartment is still empty like when i came by early this morning only this time on top of the apartment empty i find two meals in the fridge that have never been touched though beef bourguignon's her favourite

what that tells me

she's been gone since morning and never came back maybe she's been hit maybe a broken hip maybe she's in hospital maybe lost that would be worst of all if she was lost in the city wandering through streets she doesn't recognize with that worried look in her eyes and young people around laughing at her making fun at her for being lost for being not properly dressed for forgetting to put on her blouse for going about in a beige bra

no

i didn't smile

it's not funny at all

i didn't smile all by myself all alone in rose's apartment imagining her out in the streets half-naked

if that's really how it is poor old thing

for a long time now she shouldn't have been living alone that's got to change as soon as she comes back we'll have to find a place for her and if they don't want to take her I'll take her in myself my hubby bertin he'll understand all right he's my hubby bertin he'll have to understand poor old thing all alone in the city

what i do

open the coat closet by the front door open the kitchen drawers open the closets looking for clues

i've got to make sure and be certain she didn't set off into town all naked

and i have to

understand what's going on why she isn't here why she's disappeared like that

i imagine

a home invasion two men in balaclavas she opened the door all unsuspecting because with her memory she sometimes tells herself that if she doesn't recognize people it doesn't mean they're strangers and that's true no doubt about it like those days she sees me again for the first time but it could cause problems for her those two guys in balaclavas they must have dragged her out into the alley early in the morning and locked the door so the neighbour who comes by regular wouldn't be too worried so she'd think rose had just gone out to buy the newspaper like she does sometimes when she's not too bad

her newspaper that she buys from the kiosk at the metro station when she goes on the footbridge over the tracks to watch the trains go by to hear their whistle as they approach to feel the wind they make that's what she does the poor old thing in the end people get concerned

in the end they tell her to move on

they finally persuade her to leave and go home and no more will be said about it

the poor old thing comes home in a rage when that happens to her she's already lost a set of false teeth on the way home swearing at them that made her leave i had to go all the way back with her to find what had shot out of her mouth into an oily puddle close to the sidewalk and her still swearing at them that had made her leave the station with just one row of teeth to pronounce with

scoundrels

rascals

and i don't know what other insults from books i've never read but that she's been storing up since she was tiny since long before she came

another thing i do

i go into her bedroom and open the wardrobe open the drawers looking for clues

find out what's missing

is a suitcase blouses clothes several articles of clothing as if she'd set off on a trip as if she'd run away poor old thing running away where might she have gone and then i think of that dorothée she mentioned to me that dorothée i thought was just in her imagination i'm trying to reassure myself it must be that it must be that dorothée and

i take my little dishes from the fridge i'll come back tomorrow bringing nothing and the day after and from then on until she comes back the poor old thing she's long gone i wonder where she's off to how i hope dorothée wasn't just in her imagination i close the door behind me on an empty apartment poor old thing she's managed to bring me to tears and my hubby bertin was right she'll have ended up having me in tears hubby bertin how right you were

I'm the mother, inside her head, where she refuses outright.
And then there's the hay in the shed, and the baby's urine.

91

it bawls, it howls, it bawls, that's all it does: I can't take it anymore,
all those tears it soaks the white sheets with, I've no idea how to
be a mother, and Onile, poor devil, he'll never really be its father,
it was an orphan even before it grew in my womb, poor child,
when it throws a fit I feel no urge to soothe, cradle, hug, comfort;
it has to learn life's a mess, that life's full of hurt; so deal with it,
little one, cry your heart out, but deal with it, that's how life is,
full of hurt, it doesn't give you what you want, it doesn't give
you someone to console you when you need it, when you want
it, to cradle you, hug you, or comfort you, no, life takes more
from you than it ever gives back, it tears you from your love,
even a perfect one, at the risk of tearing the fibre of your heart,
of loosening the body's bonds, however strong, or if they bound
you to a lover, if they attached you to that nice pianist,
that nice pianist, with his big hands, with his long fingers, that
nice pianist with his big hands and long fingers, fingers that know
how to slide through your hair, comfort you, cradle you, grip your
wrists, open your body, who knows where to find you, when it's
hot, too hot
in the pile of hay in the barn, the neighbour's barn, that damn
barn, that barn from hell,
I remember the smell,
it was hot, and it prickled,
as usual,
like every time, it prickled my whole body, and his beard too
when he put his mouth on my neck, his mouth on my chin, his
mouth on my forehead, his mouth on my proffered bosom,
his mouth between my breasts, his mouth all over, prickling like
that, the hay too, under my body, under his weight, his reassuring
weight, the hay caught in his clothes, prickling my body through
my blouse, through the open buttons, through the skirt, just
before it was pulled up, at last, the skirt, pulled up
it prickled but it felt good, it felt good, like his beard on my body,
like his beautiful hands and the calluses that scratch, the wear and
tear of hands not meant to work in the fields, the wear and tear of
soft hands like his

I remember the smell when it happened, when I gasped with
surprise, a little
oh!
breathed, through my mouth, it was unexpected, it was the twinge,
the concern in his eyes, my smile, then his gentle eyes, reassured,
and then his hunger for my breasts, my body, his body heavy
on top of mine, pounding my hips, and the waves of sensation:
surprise, pain, satisfaction, pain, but pleasure all the same, till the
pounding stopped, too soon, just before I shuddered, a battered
lover, more from fulfillment than pleasure, my long skirt serving
as a sheet to cover our coupled bodies, despite the heat, the sweat,
the patchy comfort of the fragrant, prickly hay that padded our
makeshift marriage bed,
then the outpouring of promises, the intermingled dreams:
marriage, a house in the city, factory work, good pay, the sewing
machine and the piano, children to play the piano, like the one
they talk about on the radio all the time – a bevy of little André
Mathieus, children with long hands like his, the hands of child
pianists, restaurant dinners, dances, smoking cigarettes like grand
ladies do, and always the piano for a background, and trumpets,
and trombones, the Dixieland they play here, on this island, in the
barn, in the house we'll never buy, and in the tavern, and on the
cliff here, the tall cliff, with my breasts naked like in the hay shed,
his bare chest under his suspenders, for us to dance, even if we
fall, leaping up together to dance some more, after outpourings
ending in eternal promises, promises of shared pleasures, forever,
never mind the factory and the work-soiled hands and the kids to
be fed, forever, and dancing forever, and the constant squabbles,
so life always keeps that smell of warm hay, so warm,
I remember that smell of a man's body, of the overheated hay,
really overheated, on the verge of flames, the man's body and the
hay, that smell I'd never known, just before the afternoon rest,
my body drowsy under his caress, the only sweet moment and
the last, it was after the dancing, it was before the siesta, before
we left, separately, but seen by Juliette's prying eyes, poor Juliette,
my little sister, before little Juliette ran to Papa to say she'd seen

us, my pianist and me, in the overheated barn, spooning, poor
Juliette who'd have kept quiet if she'd known Papa would marry
me off to the Keeper,
Juliette, my little sister who I loved so much, loved like my
own child,
Juliette, the telltale child,
my last memory of him: he's running across the field behind the
village, high up where the hillside turns into the plateau, I can
see him from the barn, no one else can, that's for sure, or so
I think, he's running across the field, leaping, tossing his hat
in the air, a suspender over one shoulder, the other hanging
loose, his shirttail hanging; it was before the barn burned down:
spontaneous combustion they said, from the hay being brought
in still damp; the hay fermented, grew too hot, and blazed up,
a single burst,
when it burns like that you can only watch and wait till it
turns to ashes,
little Juliette watching me leave,
this child, this little Rose, she'll never know all that: the
lovemaking, the barn, the betrayal; that child will drag out its days
here, cut off, it'll avoid the worst, it's able to bawl already, it can
bawl all day, it can shed tears all through its room, for it is its
mother's child, it can fill a river but the river will never overflow,
for there's plenty of fish to drink her tears, and even Onile will
never catch enough of her tears,
and the white sheets blowing in the wind will dry, and anyway
tears have no smell, not like pee on the white sheets, they've no
smell or colour, not like the child's pee,
that blasted child that pees all the time, in its bed, on the sheets,
that blasted child that's never done peeing,
let it bawl away, that child, it does me good, I shouldn't think like
that, but it does me good when it bawls, that's how it is: it's like it
was crying for me
like it was crying with me
bawl, child, go on, cry your heart out, my womb is itself again,
the breeze has found my face again; bawl, child, as long as you're

crying I still exist, I really exist, I no longer feel all that pain in my
body when you let it out through your mouth,
when it's bawling I can hear it even here, the window's open,
I can hear it all the way up here, from the top of the tall cliff,
it blends into the wind, it blends into the waves, they're all bursts
of a single tumult, blending here where I too am merging,
if Onile was there, if he was back from fishing, he'd go to see the
child, he'd pick it up in his arms stinking of fish, he'd not speak
to it, but he'd gather it in his arms, carry it to the kitchen, and
that'd be it: crisis over, crying done, the child would have stopped
bawling and I'd be alone again, alone on the cliff's edge, alone in
the wind, suffering alone without existing, weeping alone, dying
alone, and he'd gather up the sheets stinking of urine and wash
them, why not, he'd wash them, and he'd gather up my shattered
body, oozing blood and sand, and wash it, of course he'd wash it.

**I'm Jacinthe, one of the almost forgotten floral sisters. She's
out of sight. There are: her barely lit cigarette, her view to
the northeast, where she keeps memories she'll never tell.
Lastly: her man-dog, Sainte-Marie, and then Sainte-Marée.**

When they started looking for Rose, I needed the open sea.
I put on my fur-lined slippers, took my pack of cigarettes off the
shelf by the front door where we put the keys, and went out on
the veranda. Then I stepped down to walk across the grass. I went
to the side of the house from where I can see the river without being
seen, neither from the house nor from the street. I'd no desire to
smoke, not at all. But I didn't want to stay in the kitchen either,
rummaging through the old-fashioned dresses of Sainte-Marie's
ghosts with Flore and Marguerite.

Earlier, on the phone with cousin Gilles, Flore couldn't contain
herself. At last something was happening in our humdrum existences,
something to add a little spice to our daily lives, now increasingly
sapped by Marguerite's failing health. She's not in good shape, Marguerite, not in good shape at all. When she limps too much, it's her
twisted body needing to find a different balance. And then her back

begins to hurt, her shoulder blade, her neck and her shoulder, and all down the arm. Then it's her mood that absorbs the pain. At times like that, all three of us suffer in silence.

But it won't pass. It won't. Not this time.

After Gilles called, Flore had the same look as when I set off for the other shore, leaving them to join my man-dog. Not that she was glad to see me go. It's just that life goes by leaving no memories behind when nothing new is happening. I think that's another reason I wanted to leave. To join my man-dog. The one who wanted me, along with my worldly goods. Even if it breaks your heart, at least when someone leaves you've got something to talk about.

When she hung up the receiver, Flore had registered everything in her spinsterly noggin. She'd registered the entire conversation so well that when she described the situation to us she repeated it all in the tiniest detail. Except that the story was twice as long, for it was embroidered with crazy notions, with her very personal stamp, with details of Gilles's tone of voice, his apparent state of health, that cough of his that made him puke his lungs. It was like always when she tells us something: she expanded it. We're used to that.

Sheltered from the world, in my little corner, out of sight and out of mind, where nothing blossoms but thoughts, I still felt no desire to smoke. I lit a cigarette all the same. From across the river the wind was carrying its load of sky across the quivering deep: impossible to see the archipelago rising up on the opposite shore. There and the edge of the world, it's one and the same.

My sisters have no notion. About those big construction sites in Sainte-Marie. They've no notion of all that's been done, altered, and invested. They'd barely recognize the village where we were born. They wouldn't *want* to recognize it.

It was when I set off for Port-Cartier with my keen, bald, young man-dog, in his big former forestry worker's pickup, that I learned about Sainte-Marée.

That week I'd been feeling at the end of my tether. I'd had enough. Enough of seeing him sprawled in front of the giant-screen TV he bought to watch hockey, every evening, every morning, on weekends, all the time. Eating afterwards, when he had the time, as if it was time he lacked. Sleeping afterwards, whenever he fell sleep, even snoring on the sofa. Wiped out in front of his big TV that he could never turn off.

I'd had enough. Enough of sinking into the same morass as him – a stone sinking a little deeper into the silt with every tide. I was suffocating in the sludge of Port-Cartier, feeding him in front of his big-screen TV: pig's trotters, spareribs, meat pies, Italian sauce – fewer than half the dishes that Flore knew how to cook for us, feeding him because it made no sense to let him die there, watching him smoke more than me, leaving traces of ash and round cigarette burns on the arms of the sofa and the leatherette ottoman. Our white and caramel apartment smelled like a charred wooden sarcophagus, a thousand-year carbonized decay. The worst of it was that more and more his touch, his kisses, turned to ash.

I needed to shake him up. I said to him: Take me somewhere, take me. We're not so far from Sainte-Marie after all, so let's go and see what's become of it after all this time, what with the changes, with folk coming and going, get yourself out, get out of that hole you're digging for yourself on the sofa, stir yourself out of your trance, quit your lethargy, I never wanted to share a coffin with you, I never wanted a grave where smoking and drinking are all that's left to life.

For he was a drinker too, my man-dog. Not too much, not all that much, but always a little. It was always on his breath. I'd had it.

He was surprised I'd talk to him like that, and it shook him up. Anyway, he washed, dabbed on some cologne, and dressed in his best duds, almost unrecognizable, to take me out and escort me wherever I wanted to go, even if it wasn't the right time of year, even if the weather wasn't great, in spite of the wind and the sudden showers on the filthy late-spring snow, despite the icy sludge that covered the sidewalks and the most uninviting roads. He did all that for me.

Up there, I saw Sainte-Marie transformed into Sainte-Marée. The village men, the youngest, the ones built like men, were assembling old houses from bits and pieces salvaged from the villages round about, every fragment numbered from the foundation to the roof, a jigsaw puzzle of a house, to give the place a different look.

First they knocked down half of the village, any houses not old or pretty enough. My sisters don't know, but our parents' house, a ramshackle cube of planks that our dad had built with the help of his brothers between two fishing trips, has been knocked down, like several others: it wasn't considered attractive enough. The kitchen where we used to eat and entertain families from around, the living room we hardly ever used, our girls' bedroom: all demolished. In its place there's an old house moved from somewhere else, Victorian in its inspiration, with a veranda all around, a little second-floor balcony, shiny metal, cedar siding, fretted mouldings, rosettes and ornamentation. And it's the same all over the village; it's been refurbished with old stuff. Old stuff moved there.

Now Sainte-Marie has become Sainte-Marée. Today's old folk, folk just like me, spin yarns to the tourists, sitting on their front porches or rocking on their verandas. Or they sell their craftwork, not too dear (but dear enough all the same): naive paintings produced on an assembly line in the sunroom; cards too, in a phony boutique called *Le Poêle*: birthday cards, postcards, playing cards, and maps drawn freehand with pen and ink; in other shops there are leather goods: belts, wallets, handbags, pencil cases, and even notebooks with leather covers studded with agates, encrusted with feathers, pine needles, and all kinds of things collected in the woods, on the plateau behind, on the beach in front, or on the islands. I bought one for my sisters, to keep all those addresses they collect.

I saw a few old friends. We greeted one another. We chatted. Drank tea. Promised to chat again. Pretended to believe we would.

I also saw some old folk I didn't know. Yet they boasted they'd been there forever, for generations. The fools hadn't twigged that I really came from the place, from Sainte-Marée. From Sainte-Marie.

On the way home, on the road to Port-Cartier in my man-dog's shining truck that he'd cleaned for the trip, my tears welled until they almost choked me. Baldy beside me was smiling with all his remaining teeth. He imagined I was weeping tears of happiness.

I tried to explain; he didn't understand a thing. As far as he was concerned I should have been glad to see everything in such good shape in the village, and smile to think I'd seen all those long-lost acquaintances again, making the most of the lovely trip he'd taken me on. An urbanite. An apartment dweller. An apartment man-dog. A guy like that doesn't understand a thing. He can yap loud enough, but he only half-listens.

I told him I was moving out the next day. That I missed the flowers. That I was going back to them, under Sainte-Euphrasie's leafy canopy. On my own.

A cowed man-dog. Incapable of biting. Just incapable – incapable of defending himself, his ideas, his desires, what he wants. Basically tame. Across from me, he began to sniffle, without uttering a word, making no attempt to keep me: a man-dog, but no watchdog. He lit a cigarette.

Back in the apartment he took off his tie and threw it away. He undid his buttons down to his navel, letting the thick chest hair stick through the opening. With his shirttails hanging out he took four beers from the fridge, two in each hand; he gripped the necks between his knuckles and stuck the bottles down between the sofa cushions next to his hip. But first he turned on the TV. Apart from helping himself to a few more bottles of beer from the pack in the bottom of the wardrobe, or going to take a pee, he didn't get up till next morning when I came out of the bedroom with my suitcase packed. He stayed stuck somewhere between the sofa and the screen while I went out to the taxi that was already waiting for me. I doubt he's budged since.

I'm a nameless village woman sitting in the lounge of an inn in Sainte-Marée, prepared to call herself anything you'd like if you're a tourist in the village. There's also Dorothée, incredulous. And the truth about the village.

We didn't have a lot to tell the tourists, we Sainte-Marie folk, and since they built a road to join the village to the 138 that loops around north of the plateau the tourists were coming more, and you had to talk to them more often, so you had to have something to tell them. We had to imagine ourselves different, we reinvented ourselves. We even changed the name of the village. Sainte-Marie was too ordinary.

The council put a guy on the job, a guy they paid to write our history, believe it or not, so we'd know what to tell the tourists. Except he wasn't a historian. No historian would ever have found anything interesting around here. A historian would rather be hanged than come looking about us. Sainte-Marie was a village just like all the others that sit the same way on the shore of the river. Sainte-Marie was a place where time passed at a snail's pace, where people died of boredom, where no one was in any hurry to get to, where folk only talked to one another because they had to. I'm telling you: just like the others, like any other village between Quebec City and Natashquan. All we could do was con the tourists who came, you understand?

We weren't unhappy in Sainte-Marie; no, not at all. It was just that we had nothing to say, nothing to tell the tourists. And then fishing's a poor way to feed a family, so a whole village, can you imagine?

They paid a writer, Caron's his name. A guy from the shore opposite, who has nothing to do with us. He'd never even set foot in the place.

Just fancy: a writer. Paid to write us a story, a different kind of story. Paid to tell us who we are. Paid to imagine us. His life's work, they say.

With the photos we found for him, he made up the whole thing. He even put his name, Caron, on the little cards in the old salting works museum, as if everything on display there was part of his work.

The wife of the lost fisherman, the one who began to sing the incantations for the husbands to come back safely, that's not from here at all. The whole thing comes from somewhere else. That's right, it's from his writer's imagination. He had to find something to fit in with the real story, with the life of our fishermen. It's thanks to Caron the village became Sainte-Marée-de-l'Incantation.

In the photos from back then the women, my dear, the women in those photos aren't doing any incantation. It's – I don't know what. If the women in the photos are up to their shins in mud, it's because they've been picking mussels. All the rest is just made up. Pap for the tourists. But it's pap that puts food on the table for us.

Pap that puts food on the table, for all of us. When the fishing's not enough.

Those incantations, if you look too hard, they don't mean a thing. Nor the rest of it neither. My dear, if you tell the truth in your movie, can you imagine? You'll be the death of this village. We'll have nothing left. So you just have to spin a yarn, like us.

We all have to spin our yarns.

> I'm the mother, inside her head, always telling herself
> the same story. There's also the official enemy, and
> Onile who takes on every countenance.

what wouldn't I give to fall asleep again, to fall asleep with you, sleep with you in the sweltering air, the two of us in a hollow in the pile of hay in the loft of old Chevillard's barn,
the air so hot, the stifling air in the barn, air almost scorching, what wouldn't I give to waken to the supple flow of your caress, your caress,
when your hands soothed the constant prickling of the hay, your hands, your long hands, that must have wanted to stroke the ivory, the hands of a pianist all your life, hands turned from their vocation, hands that can no longer undo my buttons, find my breasts to cup, nor the way beneath my skirt to part my thighs, nor untangle my hair and shake loose the hay caught in it,

your long hands that now grip only weapons, or maybe some Nazi's neck, strangling him, tightening your grip on his throat till his eyes bulge, or God knows what kind of official enemy that people learn to hate from afar and the radio calls up like a persistent ghost, a vision of bodies destined for death,
I sometimes wonder how many young German women have sacrificed their love for the good of their country, how many young German men have learned to hate us, how many have their minds reshaped, hollow cheeks, callused hands riveted to their gun, holding you in their sights as they hope to slay you, a futile hope, for you'll always be alive,

even when the body of that other bends over mine like a
husband's, I'm still back in old Chevillard's barn, lying among the
prickles, breathing in your smell and the warm scent of stored hay,
when I open my mouth, it's on your body I set it,
when I taste his body, it's your sweat in my mouth,
there's no scent in the world but yours, a scent of spice and
geraniums, and of hay clinging stubbornly to all that really exists
and the island air, always cool and damp, ceases to exist, and
the drafts that howl through the window and door frames die
away, restoring the dense silence of that old barn about our
languid bodies,

and when he's taken his pleasure, it's still you, always the you not
wanting to leave, you wanting to give me a daughter, a daughter
like me, with my eyes and my voice, you wanting to give me a
daughter, if you only knew, my Baptiste, if you only knew, over
there, that you had, then maybe you could end this war and come
back to your own country and your love, come looking for me
out on this godforsaken island with its godforsaken wireless that
just entertains us so that it can plant the war in our heads again,
at a single stroke, like a stray bullet crossing the ocean to lodge in
our skull.

**I'm a resigned tourist, meeting Rose for the first time. Also,
there'll be bread, coffee, and roses in Sainte-Euphrasie.**

Like a bombshell.
Coming suddenly face to face with that poor, lost old woman, and
her desperate eyes boring right into mine, just when I least expected it.
When I opened the door of our cabin in the Motel Pèlerins at first
light, on a morning of gummy eyelids and stifled yawns, I stepped
back and nearly fell on my butt.
I escaped
oh,
being ridiculous
oh,

gasped in like that, down in the throat, sharp, like after a punch below the belt, the kind that leaves you winded. I was on the point, yes I was, on the point of shutting the door in her face. It was the shock. But I could read the distress in her face. A remote suggestion of lucidity coming from that breathing absence standing there before me. Not the kind that allows you to understand the world around you, to be aware that it's still turning more or less the way it's supposed to, but the kind that makes us understand that we don't understand, that we no longer *know*, that if the world's still turning we're not really following, that it's casting us off into its white wake.

I said: Can I help you? That was all I could think of.

She was trying to recognize my face, something in my face – anything, some reassuring feature. I wanted to tell her not to torment herself, that it was only to be expected she wouldn't be able to place me in her memory, that she'd mistaken her door, mistaken my own cabin.

I tried to reassure her: Madame. Madame, everything's all right.

I slipped my arm into hers, just above the elbow, to make her feel all right, safe. She smiled, turned around, and went across the parking lot as if a light had suddenly come on. In spite of her bare feet she walked across the gravel, in a straight line, to another cabin over the way. She went in, and was gone.

I shut the door behind me, gently, not to waken my lover, my Marie. I went for a walk.

Yesterday evening, when we got here, we saw a little grocery store in the heart of the village, with General Store neatly painted over the door. A colour poster advertised bread baked fresh that day, every day (or so it said). Just the thing for breakfast.

Close to the motel, separated from it by just a single house, a little inn was wafting the smell of freshly brewed coffee through its screen door. I'll stop there on the way back. Maybe they'll let me borrow two cups if I promise to bring them back. People can be very obliging in little villages like Sainte-Euphrasie-de-l'Échouerie.

Along the way I'll meet: a little girl in a short skirt with a frantic dog that will burst the bubble of silence in which the village will still be adrift; an old man on his porch smoking an early-morning pipe as he rocks, giggling to himself; a teenager on his bike, riding with his hands behind his back; a man raking last year's dead leaves in front of his deserted-looking house; an old woman bending over her roses, plying her pruning shears. I won't be able to stop myself from giving her a wave. Maybe the old woman would be willing to give me one of her roses. Along with the bread and coffee, it would add some beauty to the morning.

I'll present it to my Marie. I'll present her with this rose bought from an old woman who wasn't trying to sell them. I'll tell her: You were right, it's an epic trip. Maybe you could write it into your next novel too? If you don't bleed me to death this time, it won't be so bad. And as long as you don't give everything away about my faults, my torments, heaped on the men you write about, it will be even better.

No, I won't tell her all that, I won't go that far, she'd give everything away that I want to keep between us, that's what she's like, she would for sure, she'd do it to spite me, it's inevitable. I'll give her the rose without a word, and maybe when we're leaving I'll show her where I found it, and she won't believe I managed to charm the old woman who wasn't trying to sell them. I'll give Marie the rose with barely a word; she'll be charmed, and she'll see that basically it was a good idea, that basically she was right.

She'll know I've surrendered.

I'm the mother, inside her head, sticking close to the radio, ear cocked for the long-awaited news.

they said it at last, on the radio, they said: surrender,
they said Germany has signed its surrender, so you can just
imagine: all the European castles that the enemy captured on fire,
the explosions of the ammunition heaped inside the fortifications
exploding; you can imagine: the rout of the Nazis with their big-
toothed smiles, their panic-stricken hearts, their systems in shock,
as they ignite the powder before fleeing,
you can also see: the suicided corpses of despairing Fascists, and
dead bodies, laceworks of lacerated flesh on all the roads of war

and, always against this backdrop, Germans fleeing, hiding in the
shadow of the ruins they're abandoning, wailing the jeremiads of
the defeated as they writhe in shame, constantly
fleeing,
fleeing,
you were never at the front, all this time you've been teaching
school in your own country, here at home, you never went to
war, your body was never flayed, never the fatigue and mud of
the battlefield, never the blood of others on your hands and face;
and yet, and yet you never wrote, not a single line for me, nothing
about our love, never a word about the barn, about me, about my
body arching to your touch, never a word about your desire, about
your promise of marriage, about the daughter you wanted to give
me, the one who'd be like me, about your desire to find work in the
city, to go dancing, and maybe to the theatre, to buy a machine,
not a word about all that,
just the hope inside my head,
just the pointless worry, that at some point in the war I'd find you
limbless, an amputee and a cripple, that I'd no longer find your
hands at the end of your arms, those long hands that could work
magic on my skin, on my body; nothing, not a word of all that,
just a vain hope in my mind, just a pointless worry

> **I'm the child Rose on a stormy night, a frightened Rose.
> And then there's the old dog, and Onile's curds.**

The storm is coming, disquieting. The rain batters the low cliff and
the house clinging there. It's pushing from every direction. It's like
the water you sling by the bucketful at the boardwalk to wash away
the accumulated sand, dry leaves, and patches of salt from its boards.

It's not a steady stream. It's handfuls of shot hurled against the
windows. That unrelenting roar is all there is, a blast filling the whole
space inside the house with gusts. A sound that deadens soul and
spirit, extending the rainstorm.

When there's a lull, I open my eyes. In the lightning flashes
I see Onile's old dog, a fetus curled up in the middle of the room.

Motionless but for the rise and fall as she breathes the humid air. The lightning doesn't bother her. At most she bats an eyelid when the muffled rumble turns into a real explosion. She's used to all that, Onile's dog. She's often gone shooting birds with him. A shot, a roll of thunder, it's all the same to her. She's asleep.

In the lightning flashes I see Onile bent over his jigsaw puzzle, always the same one. Three thousand fragments of a landscape bathed in the feeble, flickering light of the oil lamp. A cabin built of planks, grey among the autumn-tinged foliage such as you can make out on the coast in October. A stream in the foreground, to partially reflect the scene.

Already in those days I could become this cabin under Onile's intent gaze. I was this old half-reflected shed in a world with a wholesome smell of undergrowth, humus, dead leaves, and an overland breeze. Even though I'm about to shatter into thousands of pieces, I'm content. Onile is willing to touch me.

In the lingering light when lightning gashes the horizon and turns the whole world blue, I can see: Onile's face bent over his puzzle as if his moustache was a weight pulling his head forward; the fireplace framing a few almost extinct embers; the window, white for a moment before dimming again to a slate beaded with raindrops.

All evening I'd rock myself like that, near the table, watching the world vanish and reappear. Nothing is real anymore, except what emerges by chance. Brief moments of existence.

Until Onile's voice brings both of us back to the world: Daughter! Daughter, take some milk; go and make curd.

Then fear comes, that childish fear, an irrepressible fear that surges up as it always does. Because Mama is no longer here I'm the one who has to do the housework, so I have to make the curd. Onile is the papa of the story. I'm his daughter, I keep house for him. Our house.

Like always when he asks, I take a bowl of milk from the icebox and carry it to the workshop nearby. I set it down on the dusty workbench. I cover the bowl with a clean cloth so the cats can't dip their paws in it. If there's too much milk in the curding bowl a dark stain will spread over the centre of the cloth when it touches the creamy liquid.

I leave the bowl, the milk, and the cloth behind to be shaken by the storm, curdling the milk, leaving it thick and grainy, for Papa to mix with treacle or brown sugar in the morning.

From the workshop, the part of the island I can see makes a darker patch of night than the world on the horizon. Tomorrow, the gullies: the water off the headland, all the island's water pouring down. The shore will never be the same again, for it changes every time. It will be ravined, unfamiliar, until the next storm. Until the spring tides. Or the ice.

I shiver at each new rumble: quick, back to the house, where Papa is shifting his frame from one window to the next, stopping to gaze at points on the horizon only he can recognize. He's abandoned his puzzle. Now he's watching out for a distress signal, always a lightkeeper, though not a real one.

I return to the living room soaked through: it's my lot as the daughter in a house with no mother. In front of the feeble fire I dry my blouse and shake out my skirt, which is clinging to my thighs. I hear the reassuring crackle coming from the hearth amid the din of thunder, the laboured breathing of the dog stretched out on the floor, and Papa's voice mumbling prayers.

I'm nine, the dog is twelve; in a few months she'll be dead. Onile puts on his oilskin and goes out. He'll come home late in the night, soaked to the marrow with rain, bringing guests off the raging sea. Not for the first time.

They'll have curd with sugar for breakfast.

I'm Rose, fortunately not so young, but still too young for something like this: Onile stretched out on the ground.

Sometimes Papa sleeps like that, in any uncomfortable spot, here or there, wherever. Sprawled across the open lid of his desk, among scattered papers, notebooks, and sketches, or stretched out on the veranda, one foot on the steps, with icy skin and damp clothes, or on his side, near the hearth where only a few grey embers still crackle, or in the motionless rocking chair, chin on chest or head thrown limply back. With a bottle rolling nearby, rarely empty but never full, a bottle of rotgut, as he calls it, a bottle of foul hooch bought from the bootleggers.

Then you have to waken him. It's usually enough to nudge him gently with a toe, and he stands up without a word, goes into his bedroom, and lies down directly on the bedspread across the foot of the bed. Or else you have to shake him, gently brush his face, or stroke his hair and call him:

Papa, you must get up,

you must, get up,

you must get up, Papa,

get up!

After this gentle litany, anything can happen: Papa opening his eyes, letting out a shout, and going back to sleep there; Papa getting up urgently, rushing out to throw up over the guardrail the half-litre too much he drank the night before; Papa bounding into the kitchen with surprising zest, gargling with salt water, and setting off for his day. This time he stays put, not moving, not shivering, not speaking, his eyes half-open, his body slumped to the ground near the table where we eat. And then again, over and over:

Papa, you must get up,

you must,

get up, Papa,

I need you,

you're all I have,

I don't want you to go to the cliff,

Papa, I can't manage,

I can't manage!

Alone in the silence, I can't manage!

After the motel, I'm a worn-out Dorothée remembering Rose's body, a shaman in the night.

There's an oppressive silence inside the car. Oppressive. But it's a significant silence.

It weighs on our cheeks. Forces our lips to relax. It's from the weariness too. It was Rose's hallucinations that kept me awake.

In the room she was up, pacing tentatively around, brushing against the walls, testing them, feeling the window frames and the glass.

During the night she walked about, running her fingers over everything, muttering inaudible words, in a hypnotic state vaguely reminiscent of the recordings Henri played in the hotel a few days before. I don't know how long she wandered about the room. I opened my eyes when she began touching my face, imploring, whispering:

get up!

And some incomprehensible words, then again, whispering:

you must get up, you must, get up,

you must get up. Papa, get up!

I jumped. She stepped back. She muttered a few words, but then swallowed them again. And I, curled up in the crushed motel sheets, my whole body shivering, black on white, I felt afraid of her as she went on muttering, her eyes rolling backwards in her head.

Rose, the shaman of the Pèlerins Motel.

Rose, a shaman, her eyes finding the void.

Rose, the shaman, disturbing me, all night long. Even when she falls silent, when she returns to bed and her sleep waiting cozily there.

For a long while before I went back to sleep I continued to watch her, observing, waiting, scared. And this morning her fingermarks had jumbled the landscape beyond the windows into disjointed streaks. She was gone. She'd gotten up again after I helped her back to bed. I'd fallen asleep again.

I'm the mother with her pain. Also, there are the things she touches, the songs she sings, the things she hopes for.

my hands hurt,

I was meant to touch you, to feel you with my hands, my palms, but instead my hands hurt. It starts with the bread dough when I fold it over on the floured table, pounding it, folding it over, pounding it more, turning it over, folding it again, pounding it

some more. Between each push sharp pains shoot up my wrists,
into my elbows and my shoulders. Fold it again. Pound it some
more. It's that weak spot in my palm, on the line between the
thumb and the four fingers. I can't make a fist anymore. Maybe it's
being married. That's what it seems like,
then there's the axe. When I have to bring it down to split the
wood myself to heat this miserable shack that sits in the path of
the storm,
    split the wood, heat the stove,
to heat from early morning instead of sleeping, taking my ease
and sleeping,
    sleep, my lovely, it's not yet day
it's when before dawn Onile is already a scarcely visible dot,
or disappeared over the horizon, head bobbing on his yellow boat,
his *Juliette* as he'd baptized her long before I came on the scene –
every day when he puts out to sea a sad irony that reminds me of
my little sister and her betrayal,
    split the wood, heat the stove
sometimes when he's gone to bring in wood, the island's wood,
I think of the moment I'll see him coming back, standing on the
logs pulled along by the mare. The disappointment at seeing
him, his frame jolted by the animal straining at her collar as
she pulls along the logs to be cut up, divided, and split for next
year's heating,
thinking about next year already. Thinking we'll still be here,
that I'll still be kneading the dough, with my hands still hurting.
My disappointment at seeing him, an icicle at the end of his nose,
coming home all proud behind his mare. My disappointment
that the woods, no better than the sea, had not been able to free
me of him,
it could have happened. He could have been struck down by
some widow-maker branch. He only had to keep his eye on the
tree he'd just made shiver under the powerful blows of his axe,
as it fell. He only had to miss seeing the branch destined for him,
the widow-maker meant to grant me my freedom, that had been
growing for me forever, patiently waiting for the big maple beside

it to crack and be dragged down by its tangle of branches. Right
onto his head. Onto the back of his neck. Snapping it.
a widow-maker to show me my way back to the village,
he'll never let me leave. It would be so simple if he went
before me.

I'm the obligatory tourist seeing Paris again. Also, all those smells.

The last time we set off like this, it was for Paris. The same surprise:
bags packed, last-minute plane tickets, the same wide smile in the
half-light before sunrise. The same surprise, but without the early-
morning lay: she hadn't been as naughty, just content to shake me by
the shoulder, bringing a bowl of coffee in the other hand.

I remember blithely boarding the plane, unshaven and sleepy,
but gaga at being in love with a girl like her.

Being shaken awake on a morning too early to tell it wasn't still
night. Being roused by the gentle nudge of a hand in the half-light
and the smell of *café au lait*. Rushing to catch the plane in under
four hours. And experiencing Paris in all its complexity: the food,
the architecture, the stench of piss along the Seine, the noisy lovemaking in the little rented apartment, the Louvre swallowing and
later spewing out its thousands of tourists, the fury at getting lost,
the bottle, and her drunk – that was in the Luxembourg Gardens
of course – and then the huge, greedy carp in the pond at Versailles
and the pieces of ham sandwich we threw to watch them tumbling
over one another, and then getting drunk again, and regretting it
on the train home.

But, more precisely, that last time was before I realized she was
going to write about it all: Paris, the traffic, the café, the attic apartment, the orange chimney pots, the noisy sex, the *bateaux mouches*,
the smell of urine, the homeless people, the young partiers, the
cheese stinking up the fridge, the traffic and the shrieking sirens,
the wine, the wear and tear of the sex, the squeals of the metro
between stations, wine again, the too-small apartment, running
outside, the steep cobbled streets, gardens, getting drunk, the sex,
and ten days like that, taking in Versailles, Vincennes, Centre

Pompidou, and everything by way of museums, gilded interiors, female statues, above all going everywhere you could raise blisters on your feet – in other words all over Paris.

That was before I realized she was going to write about it all and make it into her next novel: that day we got lost, but worse; the day I got drunk, but more: the times we made love, only smuttier. That's what it had always been about: she wanted to write about us, she wanted me for a guinea pig, another of her characters. I don't want to be material for her novels again, the male hide to tan and cut her teeth on.

I want something useless. I want to skim multicoloured flies across the water, fruitlessly. I want to whip clear silk through the crystal, noisy air, uselessly. Or maybe catch a few trout. Just a few. I wouldn't ask for many, that's not important; I want to feel my hips howl in protest after battling the current for too long, my inner ears swollen from the thunder of the rapids, my ankles grazed by the rubbing of my long boots when the water grips me too tight. Grips me too tight, by the ankles.

An hour spent in a muddy river that I don't know isn't going to do me the good I need. And certainly not casting my line from the edge of the quay in some village I don't know, alongside some old guys I don't know, on a trip I'd never heard of, and never imagined, never wanted.

You can fish for capelin off the dock, she told me without batting an eyelid, with something like an affectionate smile in her voice. And worse: Since there was still room, I put your name down. She confessed.

Sitting here on a concrete block fishing, with my line in the foaming, brackish broth stirred by the river, beer and pop cans mixed with a jumble of brown seaweed. They're lined up on each side of me, an old blind guy to my left, smoking as he pretends to look at me, or maybe not look at me, smoking cigarettes he can roll without looking, naturally. This old blind guy bawls out the children who are playing, advises me on the best way to haul in the fish. He knows his stuff, the old blind guy, he really knows what he's talking about, or at least so it seems. He suggests using eyes, fish eyes for bait. It never occurs to him I don't give a damn whether I catch anything; all I wanted was a little peace and quiet.

Someone's filming us, a young black woman. I've seen her somewhere before. I think it was at the motel. She must be a tourist.

She's filming us. I'm not sure I like that. You can make pictures you take say anything you like.

> **The village of Sainte-Marée is all around, its old houses crowded together, the boardwalk along the beach, the quay, the river, and soon the sun blocked out behind the landscape. I'm Dorothée, dealing with a panic-stricken Rose.**

I no longer had any idea what to tell her, what I should make up. I was glad she'd calmed down. Now she's fallen strangely quiet again. Absorbed. Inert. I wondered what she'd recognize, what she'd lost, what had been done since her day, things she could never have imagined.

Now she's recovered her calm, standing against the handrail along the boardwalk at the beach. She's not crying now, nor screwing up her face, nor agitated. She sometimes turns round to look at the village, but turns back directly to stare into the river. So that nothing else exists in the whole world. So that everything else vanishes. She slowly advances into it with her gaze, to drown out whatever of Sainte-Marie remains in her mind. And to leave Sainte-Marée behind.

She sees the village.

She sees the river.

But the moment is all she knows.

Now she's herself again. A moment ago she was weeping, shedding bitter tears, almost raging, almost struggling. That was when I told her we'd arrived. In Sainte-Marée.

She was perplexed throughout her entire being: Sainte-Marie? she asked. Staring about her.

Then she began to deny it, vigorously: This isn't Sainte-Marie! A vigorous denial, with a brusque gesture, as if she didn't want to believe me, as if she no longer wanted to believe anything I said. She shook her head, but it wasn't just her head, it was a no uttered by her whole body, a shuddered no, an earth-shaking no in a tremor of her entire being.

I stopped filming. I was at a loss. About what I should say, or invent.

Then came her incomprehensible allegations. About houses replaced, houses stolen, things making a mysterious appearance. The Chiassons' lovely Victorian home: not their real one. And then the other one that belonged to what's his name: not the same at all. And that one. And that other one. Even the oldest houses in the village seemed to have appeared from nowhere. It was no use my assuring her that they'd always been there, that they'd remained almost unchanged, I just managed to enrage her further.

Now she's facing the river. I was able to calm her, holding her in my arms, murmuring in her ear,

shh, it's all right,

shh, you can see, everything's fine,

shh, Rose, you're right,

easy, calm down, it's all fine,

you're right.

Now she's calmed down, standing close to me against the handrail along the boardwalk at the beach. She's no longer crying, no longer screwing up her face, no longer upset. She's gripping the handrail in front of us.

The village women are advancing slowly on the shore, barefoot; one by one they roll up the hems of their dresses to mid-thigh, or draw them up between their legs to their midriffs. It's about to start, at last.

It's sure to do Rose good.

There are more and more of them. I can count more than a score. Young women, but very few children. Most of the young girls have hung back. They'll hum along too, but from a distance. They've come to learn how it's done: that's the way traditions get passed on.

The first woman advances into the silt along the river's edge, then up to her knees in the brine, and then up to her thighs among the seaweed and mosses. Her hair hangs loose. There's salt water on her dress. Since she's facing the open water, you can't hear her, but she has already begun her chant. It's a strange prayer.

It's a harmony I could listen to forever. The women follow her on the shore, at the water's edge and into the waves, striking up a deeply moving canon, *a cappella,* a changing mantra in the surf, passed from mouth to mouth, from misfortune to misfortune, a canon more powerful than all the foghorns that have resounded across the river. Here and there a voice stands out, but it is soon lost among the others and in the roar of the surf. There are young married women, old women, and widows, all joining in the incantation. Their bodies sway in the water churned up by the uneven breakers: their shoulders sway in a shared languor. It's a show put on for the tourists, of course, but you can sense that the village women still perform it with passion. Offered up like this to the river's lip, they would willingly be swallowed up to keep their menfolk safe, for all their men to come home. They're imploring the sea to spare their loved ones, their families. To take *them* instead, to avoid the worst.

They say it was a young widow who began the incantation a little more than a century ago after her husband was lost somewhere off the headland where Keeper Onile finally settled. Brouillard himself was supposed to be descended from one of the men swallowed by the river. That's part of his legend.

The first woman was a bit odd, they say. She must have been, no doubt about it. With the river water up to her hips, she didn't cry out her despair. She chanted, gently, gripped by the waves, repeating her pagan ritual whenever the village men were setting out to sea. It finally dawned on them that she wasn't crazy. That she was praying for the others, for the village fishermen, so that they wouldn't be taken like her man: Take me instead of another of our men, I'm ready, take me instead of another one. That she was praying for others, for the village women, and soon they joined her, barefoot in the brine, carrying their daughters in their arms: Take me instead of another of our men, take me instead of another lover, take us instead of our fathers, we're ready, take us all for them to come home.

As soon as the first women approached, I raised my camera to my shoulder and filmed the scene. Now Rose has calmed down. I'll have a record of it. As for the incantation, I've filmed it already. But this is an important day, and it's an important moment: I focus my lens on the features of the old woman beside me. In the background the women are moving beyond past the damp shore, where the shingle is lifted by the eddies at the edge. I want to record her reaction. To miss nothing of her keen attention.

Rose turns to me: What are they doing?

I'm the flyfisher-become-tourist, the one who'd rather be somewhere else. With him, a Marie, a highly persuasive lover; around them is a museum that would like to be bigger. There are also a few surprising clues.

Did you notice? I ask her.
Yes, no, maybe.
She hasn't a clue what I'm talking about, her eyes swing from one spot to another, half-curious, half-indifferent, bouncing off the various objects displayed with the pretension of a museum that thinks itself bigger than it really is. The room is large and white with wooden beams of impressive girth across it, a reminder that not very long ago trees of that size reached skyward in the woodlands on the plateau and around.

I try to explain to her. There are inconsistencies. Incongruous details. There, look. And I point a discreet finger to the thing that had jumped out at me.

It was in a modest display cabinet between the eastern wall and one of those imposing wooden beams, a Plexiglas cube scuffed by tourists' fingers. Or by their looking through it. Just an ordinary cigarette box. When only the best will do, proclaims the inside of the lid, which is held open by a spot of transparent wax. It's a box made of red, gilded metal, rusty, containing square nails of various sizes laid in rows running in the same direction as the cigarettes once did.

She still hasn't caught on. On the card beside the object, its description reads:

Metal box, gilt detail (9 × 7.6 × 1.8 cm).

Originally contained twenty cigarettes manufactured by Benson &
Hedges, Superior Virginia Cigarettes, Old Bond St., London. Probable
date of manufacture: between 1940 and 1945. Made in England.

Lower down on the card, its history:

This cigarette box was found with its contents in the house of Onile
Brouillard, known as the Keeper, during the recent restoration by
Plumules Nord Ltée, the ecotourism development company. It was
probably purchased in the early 1940s, probably by Laurent Bataille,
the apprentice to the legendary fisherman, shortly before he left
for the war.

Then there are a few words about the nails it contains.
She whispers that she finds it all extremely interesting, but makes
as if to head off towards another exhibit.

> **I'm an angler-tourist's Marie. There's her husband,**
> **who infuriates her. It happens in the silence of an**
> **exhibition room of the Sainte-Marée museum.**

The room is empty of people. If it wasn't for a few videos running
in a loop, their muted accompanying commentary coming from the
headphones, the silence would be perfect and intimidating. Apart
from the sighs of the receptionist as she flicks through the pages of
a catalogue.

I don't know what's gotten into him, acting like a museum
inspector. I tell him in a whisper that his concern is fascinating, but
I want to move on.

> **I'm the angler-cum-tourist-cum-museum inspector.**
> **He's trying to be patient with his Marie until she**
> **understands what his intuition was about.**

She hasn't got it. I explain it to her. That I have the very same
thing at home. In my office. That I thought it was old when I found

it in my workshop wall. That I did some research to find out what it was worth. Not a red cent! It's funny that today they're using it for what? To hold a few rusty, bent nails!

I show her the card again. It says it was made in the early 1940s. It couldn't have been bought then. Never mind that it's made of metal, is a bit rusty, and looks old – which is simply not possible. It was in the 1980s that those boxes of twenty cigarettes were sold, I'd swear. That was long after the Keeper's house was abandoned. That is, if you can believe anything they tell you here.

She tells me that's enough. That I'm being disingenuous. That I'm mistaken. That it's impossible. That it's a simple error. She wants me to change my attitude. Because it's becoming tiresome. She'd like me to be a bit more positive. Because I'm spoiling our holiday.

I'm spoiling our holiday.

But the thing is, she hasn't noticed anything else.

That photo. Which is known to have been taken in 1973. The one that had absolutely no intention of showing what I noticed, but was just meant to be a shot of men fishing off the dock, taken from the deck of a boat, the anglers smiling broadly with their tackle and buckets of capelin beside them. And that's what you see if it's the only thing you look at; that's what it intended to show: happy anglers and great fishing.

But behind, from that angle, behind the men fishing, behind the smiles, the rods, the hooks, and the buckets of fish, you can also see the village. And it doesn't have half the century-old houses that stand there today. So I say to her:

Look at this photo. You get a great view of the village, don't you?

Then her eyes scanning the picture in the frame. Her eyes widening.

I'm Dorothée on the quay, with Rose standing there patiently, those two tourists setting out to experience for two nights what it's like to live on an island, the photographer sent by Plumules Nord, and the captain of the boat that will take them all to the island. Also visible is the boat with *Le Passeur* inscribed in neat letters on its hull, at the prow.

The captain of the boat has just tied up *Le Passeur* to the jetty. He's Émile. A man of few words.

I don't know the photographer personally, just in passing. He's been sent by Plumules Nord, my company, for that was the objective of all my efforts to find Rose: to obtain some striking pictures. On the phone, Jérôme, the one with the beard and the crook-toothed smile, waxed more than enthusiastic, offering me a bonus, inviting me to dinner, asking me to think about what I'd enjoy most. Though his enthusiasm evaporated when, most likely with a fingertip planted in his daybook, pointing at the date of some conference taking place in the capital, he realized he couldn't be there in person.

It was the same photographer who'd come during the work on the island. He's the one who usually takes all the pictures for Plumules Nord. He's not much of a talker either. I don't know much about him, I've never been able to get more than a few words out of him. It'll be a fun crossing, that's for sure.

He took a few shots. Rose co-operated most willingly. I was filming: the boat as it arrived and then as it rocked peacefully on the swell; the captain tying up to the quay; the crewman's smile as he rolled out the gangway before inviting us on board, one at a time, taking the ladies by the hand and the men by the forearm.

I'm feverish. Finally, Rose is about to see: the island, what it's become; the Keeper's house, her house, shining like the stones at the river's edge when they're wet, when they're gleaming after the tide, when their livelier colours attract the eye; all the restoration work we've done, the furniture repaired, touched up, replaced, relocated; the beaming faces of the visiting tourists.

Naturally I won't tell her about: the rot that had taken hold in the walls to the north and in the roof space; the leaks that obliged us to replace the metal roof, to remove it and give it a steeper slope; the furniture and the wallboards that had all been used for firewood by the squatter who spent several winters there, or his shoddy insulation job, which did more harm than good because he didn't know what he was doing; the bottles of booze piled up in one of the bedrooms – beer, homemade wine, white rum, and cheap brandy, or the smell of moonshine that had gradually permeated the premises over time, and then the wasps, dozens, hundreds of them, inside the house; they'd built a nest in the western wall as well as in the crawl space under the roof. All the work needed to get rid of them. The boards ripped out at nightfall, the cans of insecticide, the instinctive fear of the little beasts, the race to the river to shake off the brutes, the way it hurts when they plant their stinger in you! I won't tell her all that. She doesn't need to know everything. Absolutely not.

I'll tell her what she'd like to hear: it was so easy to renovate your father's house, so well built for its time, so solid. We just had to do it up a bit, freshen the paint, hang new curtains in the windows. I'll tell it the way the guys hired by the company tell it to the visitors: that this house was constructed to stand in this landscape, so that no storms on the river could ever shake it. Not even storms from much farther away.

Or maybe I'll change my mind – maybe I won't lie to her, but just not tell her anything. Maybe there's no need to say anything.

A couple of tourists join us on board; they hand their numbered tickets to Captain Émile. They're going to make the crossing with us and spend the night on the island. They don't speak, never look at each other, never touch.

The man was fishing for capelin yesterday, when the tide was coming in. He has a vacant expression. When he looks at you it's with an emptiness that wants to swallow you up.

The woman's quite beautiful. She's taking notes and photographs. In her black notebook:

Émile, the captain of the Passeur.

Morning overcast, but fairly warm.

You can sense that the wind will soon alter the quality of the light. There are sharp spurs of sunlight on the river, predicting the change.

And I don't know what else. She shut her notebook as soon as Captain Émile invited us on board with his affable manner.

All throughout the voyage he pretends to be trying to seduce the female tourist. Once the boat is cruising at a decent speed he assumes an alarmed expression, turns off the engine, and loudly advises the passengers, as if there's an emergency: Keep calm, everyone, hold tight to the gunwales! Come on, crew! He unhooks the mouthpiece from his radio and sends a distress call, announcing earnestly to his interlocutor: SOS, I'm lost. Then he explains, with a glance towards the crew: There's a siren on board! SOS!

Rose remains expressionless, but the female tourist is amused by this character who's conveying them on his boat, and she is charmed by this compliment clearly aimed at her.

Captain Émile chats more than usual, boasting that he has the finest boat in the village, the most stable, the longest. Of course, he says, I've always picked the right candidate.

Here and there he points out a whale's back, a seal's head, terns swooping, guillemots, whatever he notices, always addressing the woman he continues to refer to as his siren, and slowing down to satisfy the tourists' curiosity. For that's the way it's supposed to be.

And all this time Rose continues to pose for the photographer's persistent lens.

I'm Rose in the lacklustre eye of the unceremonious photographer, Rose, with a meek smile, reconquering her territory.

On the quay before boarding the *Passeur*.

On deck with the wind in my hair, messing it up.

Still on deck, with the captain of the *Passeur*, all proud to know who I am.

On the bridge again, watching the archipelago rise up. I'm smiling.

The moment when I see the house appear on the little cliff. Emotional.

Near the jetty, still on the deck, about to go ashore.

On the boardwalk, leaning on the railing with its saltire balusters. Gazing towards the open water, shoulders turned east-west.

On the big staircase, seen from below, me going up.

On the big staircase, again, me going up, this time seen from above. That was just after the photographer ran up, getting out of breath before me.

He's all around me with his picture-taker, snapping my picture, saying: Do this. Do that. A little more like that. But mostly not saying anything. It doesn't mean he's discreet, for he often sticks his lens right in my face. Reassurances from Dorothée, the African girl: Don't worry about him, everything will be fine, he's very nice.

It's true he's nice, the photographer. And while I'm posing for him, Baudelaire's cat is filming me. Here, everything is *luxe, calme, et volupté*. I feel important.

At the top of the steps, I'm ageless. Everything is still new, nothing has changed since I left. Time hasn't been kind to me, but it has left this place just as it was. Onile could come out of the house this very minute and I wouldn't be surprised. Or his yellow boat could appear on the horizon, laden with the nets he's hauled aboard.

This is where he would stand most often to scan the river. Before he raised his spyglass he'd lean his shoulder against the corner of the house to steady it. It was also where he used to sit to have a better view of my comings and goings. Coming back from the garden higher up. From the workshop nearby. From the peninsula. From the shore.

You can see a long way, it's true. From here there's a view over every island in the archipelago. Not all of them exist when you're standing on the shore.

I'm Rose, aged twelve, tracing aerial links over the open water between the islands, connecting them.

At the top of the steps: I'm twelve, it's all new; so is my view of the landscape. I'd like to build a bridge between the islands, I'd cross it often, I'd go to the other side.

I'd go across, running as fast as my little feet of a girl not yet a woman could carry me, I'd reach the island opposite without getting wet, so I could see everything differently. To see that my island, my own island, is tiny. To see that my house is even tinier. And that when I'm on my island, in my house, I too am tiny. That my insignificant misfortunes as a girl almost a woman, my trifling misfortunes as a girl with no mother to show her the way, my own trivial misfortunes, don't matter to the world.

If there was a bridge between the house and Hare Island, I'd cross it, to see the world differently. So that I could realize that everything is just the same from the other side. That a bridge between two islands always means a return trip, just a gap between two shores. Between two beaches, two samenesses.

It would help me realize that differences don't exist all that much.

If there was a bridge between the house and Hare Island, it would be a steel one, like the one in Quebec City. It would be green too. I can't imagine it any other way. And it would be dotted with rivets – including a gold one, for the legend. And it would have collapsed twice during the construction. A heap of twisted metal. And bodies. The bodies of fathers. Of uncles, brothers, cousins. The bodies of Native Americans with no fear of heights.

It too would have collapsed twice, my bridge. Carrying my fathers, uncles, brothers, and cousins down with it. Native Americans with no fear of heights. The bridge between my islands. The bridge I'd be able to build.

If there was a bridge between the house and Hare Island, there would have been men to cross it. Men jingling coins in their pockets as they went across. For a long time I'd have watched them coming, hoping it was young Bourgeois, the delivery boy. The one I watch from behind the hazel bush near the balustrade when he goes along the boardwalk carrying Papa's order. I watch him, a dream in my eyes and in my belly, like the sun.

I'm young Bourgeois remembering how he landed in Rose's life and changed it for her. Also, the Brouillard girl suddenly has a name.

I used to go there like that every second week. Monsieur Brouillard would make me a list, and I'd make sure I found everything for him before the next time. That week the order was almost complete, there was just one book short, I don't remember which, but that often happened with books, especially the most sensitive ones, the ones that aren't supposed to be sold, but Monsieur Brouillard never got upset. When the one he wanted came, he'd order another one automatically. I suppose that gave him time to read.

The important thing is that everything else was there. Monsieur Brouillard would be pleased. When he was pleased, he'd say to me:

Bourgeois my boy, you're a good messenger, much better than your hopeless father, who forgets everything. Monsieur Brouillard often told me he was pleased.

When I got there, there was nothing moving on Keeper's Island, even less than usual. There was hardly any wind, and if it wasn't for the motion of the waves you'd have thought you were looking at a photograph. A colour photograph. It was lovely. That's something you didn't often see in Sainte-Marie in those days, a colour photograph.

When I got there I had to tie up the boat, heave the wooden crate onto the dock with a shove of my hip, step ashore, and hoist it onto my shoulder. When I tried to lift it all the way, the crate tumbled right over.

On the beach, a hundred feet away, stock-still, there was the Brouillard girl, the island's daughter. She was sitting with her arms round her knees, staring out to sea. She was partly responsible for my screw-up, for she'd startled me: I couldn't have expected to see her there. In fact I never saw her at all. She always kept well out of sight when I came.

No one ever saw her. Me no more than anyone else. Except occasionally, when she'd crouch behind the hazel bush. I'd let on I hadn't seen her.

When I saw her so close, and out in the open like that, I was surprised. The crate literally flew over my shoulder and dumped all its contents on the boardwalk. The milk bottle exploded, soaking the newspapers. Everything else seemed okay, I could thank my lucky stars.

With the racket I made, the girl on the beach turned towards me. She was alone, and dirty, and crying hard. When she saw me she began to howl like one possessed, and then she ran towards the steps and up them like a frightened rabbit and went and shut herself up in the house. As for me, I picked up the crate and everything I could salvage. It was none of my business how she carried on, that one. I'd just have to say I was sorry about the milk. I could bring two bottles next time, to make up for it. As for the newspaper, it was too bad. Fortunately the bottle of brandy was intact. I didn't think

Monsieur Brouillard would be upset with me. They could manage without the milk. And the news. The brandy was another story.

Except that Monsieur Brouillard was nowhere in sight. His boat was there, and so was his mare, but there was no sign of him. When I'd knocked long enough on the door, the island girl opened it. She was shaking like a leaf in the doorway, straight, as if she didn't want to allow me in. She'd changed her blouse, tried to clean up her face. There was still dirt under her nails and filth on her neck and her forehead, but you could see she'd tried to look clean. Her eyes were red, like a girl trying to keep from bawling.

I asked her where her father was. She just answered, sobbing, that he wouldn't be coming back. And when I asked about her mother, she looked puzzled. Then she dissolved into tears – a real collapse. I understood that her mother wasn't there either.

It was me brought her to the village, the Brouillard girl. She needed some convincing, but I couldn't very well leave her there all alone, not in the state she was in. When I got her home, the poor girl, Mama washed her. We were sent outside. I kept an eye on the youngest ones in case they tried to peep through the glass in the door. But I saw. She was all skin and bones, poor thing, all scrawny. She cried all the time. She was afraid of everyone but my mother. That was why she looked after her, the Brouillard girl.

Rose was her name. Rose Brouillard.

After one or two weeks living with us, when she was doing better, when she wasn't so scared, we had to look about finding her a place somewhere else. It wasn't quite right for her to stay on, what with me and my brother in the house.

That's what the meeting was about. My father was there. When you own the general store your opinion counts. What's more, he looked after the village money, and was in the parish guard. That meant he belonged on the committee. Other folk from the village were on it too. The *curé*, of course. It was to discuss what they could do for her. They offered her a future somewhere else. I think they sent her to Montreal. They found her a job as a seamstress. She knew how to use a sewing machine – they had one on Keeper's Island, for I often had to deliver cloth. She was capable.

125

She left by boat. In those days it was the fastest way. She never went back to the island, she just left it all the way it was.

I'm an elderly Rose in an apparently stable world. And everything there is.

They're busy around me, dealing with the luggage. There are so many people. A man and a woman, looking like lovers, whispering together but never touching. A young black woman who's willing to take my arm. A photographer turned in my direction. And another man, in overalls and a long-sleeved white sweater, with a thick moustache under his nose, clutching his beret in his fist to say goodbye. He's casting off his yellow boat, ready to leave. The photographer takes the opportunity to snap a few pictures of him standing in front of his boat.

I'm an old woman. They want to help me go in. Below, there's no hazel bush. No Bourgeois boy to walk to here.

I'm the twelve-year-old Rose, with the stories in her head. Lots of people too.

If there was a bridge between the house and Hare Island, there'd be lots of people to cross it. Visitors. Native Americans with a bevy of kids. Maybe a train. Trucks. Like the ones sitting around in the villages. Cars too. With fathers, uncles, brothers, and cousins in them. Family I have, but don't know.

All the family I have. Who don't know me.

As if the bridge I built between the islands had collapsed one day and dragged them all down into the gap. Leaving me without any ancestors. Without any descendants.

I'm Rose who's never had a child except herself, and who finds a shred of meaning somewhere in the links between the islands.

If there'd been a bridge between the house and the islands, maybe I'd never have left. But there's never been a bridge between the islands. Since forever, and more than ever, they're disconnected. They float apart. Helpless vessels. Wrecks. Aground. With birds flocking around them. Eider ducks acting dumb. Terns diving. Beating down greedily on the shoals of fish.

The islands are dropped words, outstripping thought. Like splattered chapters. Heading in every direction.

If there was a bridge between the islands, my memories would be linked. For I've got all these islands inside my head. I can't invent bridges between them anymore. I need to sit down. Dorothée's still there; she's real. She can support me, help me inside. In one corner of the house, standing at attention in front of us, a sentinel, silent in spite of itself.

The gramophone from back then. It's still in the same place, ruddy, massive, upright, with rounded corners. Dorothée opens the lid. A thick record is placed on the turntable. As if it had never budged from its spot. If the spring in its mechanism had survived the years it could play again at last.

I'm Onile the assistant keeper, still a young man. Young Onile is assistant to a real keeper, and he knows the hardships of the Brandy Pot light: kerosene, cannon shots, and all that.

I was too close to the muzzle, too close. Now, in the fog, there are no more waves, no more wind, no more sound, just a monotonous, endless ringing. The Brandy Pot will have done for my hearing.

Yet they'd told me to watch out. He'd told me, Gérard, the Brandy Pot lightkeeper.

The gun stopped up my ears, a cannon shot to my eardrums. Killing, at one fell swoop, everything that sings, resonates, and delights, or starts you dancing. It killed silence too; from now on there'd be none, it was broken forever.

I'm young Onile, Gérard's assistant, only even here I'll be less useful now.

**I'm Onile the fisherman and the papa of the story,
Onile with ears that hurt, unable to hear, or sometimes
hearing too much, both too loud and too much.**

The world's too noisy, it raises an unrelenting din that leaves an enduring echo inside my head. The flag on the *Juliette* has been flapping in the wind all day, irritating. I'm sapped within, weary of this ringing pain that sets a bar in the base of my skull.

She put on a record. The child loves music, so she turned the handle, wound up the spring, and started the music booming, a stabbing pain in my head. A confused mess of inaudible or distorted sounds. A hopeless succession of strangled melodies. I can only distinguish a distorted, painful, auditory impression.

She's listening, she's dancing, I can't stand it any longer, I close the lid.

The little rebel winds up the mechanism again. She refuses to close the front panels to reduce the volume. It hurts in my ears, in my skull, inside my head, but she won't close the panel. For she's strong-willed, this little one. So I have to lose my temper, take back the key to the machine and put it away in my desk where she can't get it again, can't stab my earholes, for her to stop injecting that same piercing, persistent note into my silence. I can hear her crying. I'm used to that. It won't hurt so badly as long as she doesn't start to bawl.

In the completely renovated Keeper's house, I'm a naked woman speaking to her mate, who's stretched out on the bed, taking advantage of the light entering through the panes to indulge in the sight of his blue-tinted body. There's a full moon over Keeper's Island.

There's something touching about that old lady, I find. It's the way she looks at everything around her. Her tears. We're lucky to be here at the same time as her. Don't you think? What I mean is, even if they do dress up the truth a bit in the village, we're pretty comfortable here, it's an interesting spot.

Listen, can you hear? It's so quiet on the islands. I think it was worth it.

Come. Take me in your arms, don't you want to? I'm happy.

I'd like you to know that I'm glad to be here with you. I would have been glad somewhere else too. But this is better. I'd begun to miss those sudden whims. It seems to me we used to be more spontaneous, more daring in our impulses. I think there was less restraint in our relationship. Less calculation. Now we calculate everything. Ration everything out. It's since the kids, probably. They've taught us to calculate and measure things long before they could themselves.

I'm glad to be here with you. That you came here with me. I needed that.

Not the trip.

Not this village, not that lying museum, not the beach, not the performance, not even this night in an old house on an island. That's all very fine, but it's neither here nor there.

I know what you think, I get it. But I didn't come here to write, it wasn't to write, not now, nor later. I never intended that. It's just that things we experience sometimes leach down into my fingers all by themselves, and there's not much I can do about it. But that's not why I'm here, it's not why I brought you here, I've no desire at all to write about it, and if anyone does, it won't be me.

I needed, just needed, I really needed for you to come along. That's all. For you to join me in some crazy thing, no matter what, it could have been anywhere. We could have stayed shut up in our bedroom for the whole week, both of us naked – why not? You'd have looked at me just the way you look at me here, the way you watch me at the window when I'm pretending not to notice. We could have done all that at home, making love and so on. But it's always easier to go away. It seems like it's better to be naked somewhere else.

It's nice, being naked here.

Do you think they could hear us? The walls are just boards. You can feel the wind from outside. What's inside can't have gone unheard.

It's a bright night. Have you noticed? Have you seen how bright the night sky is here? At home, even when there's a full moon like that, the night is never more than dull, flooded the way it is with the sodium-yellow street lights. Here it's different: it's blue, it's bright. You can see the shadows of the buildings on the ground. I'm sure you could go for a walk outside without a flashlight. Not far, you can never go very far on an island. But for a good while, yes.

You could walk for a good while by moonlight. Until morning. In the wind outdoors.

I'm Dorothée about to panic one morning on Keeper's Island. While the tourists' bliss grows stronger in a three-fingered embrace.

I thought she was asleep, that she was sound asleep in the room that was hers as a little girl. That she was just asleep.

I thought after all that travelling she must be worn out. I mean the drive, that long drive from Montreal, and all the emotion too, for she's experienced some powerful emotions since she left Montreal. I really thought she was still asleep.

Captain Émile came by first thing bringing a basket with the nosh for the tourists: croissants for breakfast, duck pâté, red pepper and walnut jelly; sandwiches for lunch, baker's bread – a lovely smelling crusty loaf, apple-wood smoked ham, local cheddar, rose jelly with petals, coffee, of course, a full Thermos, and a bottle of red wine. When I got up, the two tourists were drinking their coffee, sitting on the veranda, inhaling the sea air.

They look like lovers this morning. Much more than yesterday. The night's rest, no doubt. Or something else, you might imagine. He's holding three of her fingers, from the first to the ring finger in his loosely closed hand, like a handful of shiny glass marbles he was observing attentively. It's a discreet embrace exchanged between their two drawn-together chairs.

They know I work for Plumules Nord – I haven't hidden the fact. They asked me if it's possible to explore the island, all of it. I reassure them: the eiders' nesting season ended in early July, so the trails round the island to the west have been reopened to the public. But you have to keep to the established paths to avoid trampling the vegetation. Some areas are closed off permanently. I explain that if all the tourists that come were allowed to tramp over the forest soil the island would be bare rock in a few years. It would end up like Haiti: deforested, naked. That made them smile.

The map pinned to the wall inside is detailed. I invite them to follow me, and I show them the areas to avoid. They're still holding hands. Whispering. Bursting out laughing. Whispering again. Laughing again. They return to sit in the open air. It's a lovely morning by the river, with a pleasant odour of distant humidity, wisps of iodized mist rising round about, and the banal contentment of a couple at their ease.

Alone again, I pour myself a coffee. I tear a croissant apart and spread it with the rich pâté and spicy jelly.

Later I go out to stroll along the bank, set foot on the jetty, and gaze out to sea, hoping to spot something, anything at all. While the buildings were being renovated we often saw the snouts of curious seals, or their shiny bellies upturned to the sun, belugas raising white bulges on the river's opaque surface, bigger whales to the east-southeast, and huge cargo ships with the tranquil air they maintain through the higher waves in the distance.

The two tourists continue to whisper together, saying holiday things to each other, things people don't usually say but that occur to them when they're able to halt the passage of time. If I see something, I'll point it out to them. That'll make them happy.

The river is calm. I should have brought my camera, even though Rose isn't up yet. To take the landscape where she's sleeping once again. I should have.

I wonder if she's okay. I'm surprised she's sleeping so late, though she was obviously worn out yesterday evening. Our two nights together in Sainte-Euphrasie and in the inn at Sainte-Marée both ended early. It's strange she should drag this one out so long.

Then the nightmare occurred to me: she has died in her sleep, it's all been too much for her; I've killed her by taking her away from home. What was I thinking, what possessed me to have taken her away from her quiet life, to confront her with the burden of her past, to have forced this expedition on her, far from her home comforts, far from her reassuring notes to herself? Poor old woman! Being brought back to her past like this. Such a brutal reversion.

The worst nightmare of all: to find her old woman's body half-naked, half-out of the bed, half-alive, on an island half out of sight, isolated, thirty minutes from the nearest boat captain, Captain Émile, who this very moment is hiring out his yellow motorboat to bring some tourists to see the pod of whales that are basking some fifty kilometres offshore.

I rush back the way I came, climbing the long steps slung along the low cliff that lead to the house, then up the stairs to the bedroom where Rose must be sleeping like a log.

I knock.
No answer.
I go in.
Empty.
There's no one in the unmade bed.
There's no one in the rocking chair, which is sitting motionless near the window.
No one.

Rose. She must have taken off during the night, like at the motel in Sainte-Euphrasie. It's probably fatigue from the drive, that long trip from Montreal. The emotion too, the powerful emotions she's been subjected to since we left Montreal. I'm responsible.

I have to get a grip. Think. Be efficient. Not lose my bearings in the turmoil that's confusing my thoughts. Do something. Rose.

Maybe she went out in the middle of the night to go somewhere, to some spot she's known forever, to do things she used to do long ago, to imagine an already familiar world and throw herself headlong into it, taking advantage of our being asleep, me and the tourists, to recover her bearings.

I thought she was asleep, sound asleep, in the room she slept in as a little girl. That she was simply asleep. Now she's lost, on an island she knows much better than I do.

I'm a tourist able to keep a cool head. There's that lost old woman. A search party is organized on the island.

The map pinned on the wall until a moment ago has been taken down and spread out on the table. As we look on, the young woman from Plumules Nord divides up the island with a fingertip, pointing out the most likely dangers, the ground we have to cover, the paths for each of us to follow. She called up the mainland on the radio, but no one will get here for at least half an hour. We'll be well along with our search before then.

She's going to set out straight through the little woods, along the path used by the workers who go to the western end of the island to collect down from the eiders' nesting ground on the point. We're to go along the shore, each in our own direction.

In my case I'll head north, go up onto the cliff and search the nearby places, the buildings and the landscaped areas. According to her, there are supposed to be long, overgrown trails that the old woman might know. If I look closely I should be able to see them.

Marie is to follow the south shore. She can follow it to the western point and then return along the path created for the tourists, with viewpoints and several boardwalks.

Above all we have to remember that if we get lost on the island we should walk south, always directly south. On the northern shore the terrain is difficult, fractured by cliffs and ravines. The southern sector is easier going.

In our pockets each of us carries an emergency blanket in a water-proof envelope, matches, a candle, a flashlight, and a distress flare.

Ahead of each is our own route, to be followed from memory. With only one map among the three of us, it was left on the kitchen table.

It could have been predicted that she'd get lost, that old woman. That she'd escape. That she'd wander off and disappear. It was inevitable.

But, on the other hand, what I didn't foresee was this interval of solitude that'll do me a lot of good. The peace of the island. Without her beside me, without a Marie trying to monopolize my attention. Just to be in the world, face-to-face with it, to be the one for whom the world exists. If I'd only had my mouth organ in my pocket this sudden happiness would have been perfect. I'd have played a tune as I went, to make the world exist differently. Then she'd have heard me coming, Rose, the lost lady that I'd have been able to make reappear, a dancing old woman.

I'd really like to find her, this Madame Brouillard. Except I'd rather not see her dead. I've never seen a dead body, except for my father in his casket, made up to look almost alive, choked by his too-tight collar and tie, his head resting on the cushion of cream-coloured satin that didn't really suit him. But a real dead body, someone just gone, bloody and blue, that's something I've never experienced. So I've absolutely no wish to find Rose, this aged Rose, with her body all scraped and broken, on the rocks at the water's edge or hanging in the branches. I'd rather she gave me a scare, suddenly coming face to face at a bend in the path, on the other side of a tree, like on the other side of a motel cabin door, or between two enormous stones gathered against each other at the foot of a cliff, safe from everything and everyone.

Marie set off on her path along the shore like a woman possessed. This must be a marvellous holiday for her. She left with notebook in hand, on her way to save a life: that's her ambition. That's her, humming a lively tune, refusing to fear the worst, refusing even to imagine the worst she could fear.

As for the employee, she looked haggard and panicky. I think she was blaming herself, poor girl.

So I'm searching. The only harmonica is the one playing inside my head, even more plaintively than anything I might have improvised if my instrument hadn't been left in the glove compartment of the car.

I'm searching, walking without conviction.

A deserted shore, as far as the eye can see.

The tide's going out. What it leaves behind on the shingle: an undulating line of seaweed, mosses, and seashells.

A gull pecking at the shell of a tiny crab, harassed by three of its own kind.

A cliff with one foot on the beach, plunging its other foot into the water farther on.

A minuscule peninsula linked to the shore by a vague line of stones it must be possible to walk across at low tide.

There, on the stones, a brownish stain. I wonder if it's blood. I'm worried. I look around.

I find nothing.

I find no one.

I'm relieved.

Now I've had enough of being here. I no longer have any desire to search. I'd much rather sit on the damp beach, gazing into space for anything that turns up. Seabirds, foam, boats ... But I keep walking, searching, heading up the steps to get back onto the little cliff where the house stands. There: the buildings, doors are locked, but for a decrepit shed that I peek into before investigating the old buildings.

I find nothing, no one.

I'm relieved.

Then, round about, lifting the foliage, moving the branches, observing, listening. With the wind that's blowing, an old woman in tears doesn't make much sound. I must stay alert.

I try to remember her old woman's scent. Eyes closed, I sniff the wind that reaches me. I can't smell anything except that river smell that clings to your nostrils when you're not used to it.

I found this long branch I can use to flatten out the grass, push aside the leaves, and to break other branches. She's nowhere to be found.

But there, behind the shed, isn't that one of those old paths the employee told me about? Perhaps someone went that way. Or was it me, just now, that broke that branch? I venture along it, the end of my stick in front of me, testing the ground. Eventually I reach a clearing where some long-neglected perennials are growing, choking one another out. There's a jumble of wildflowers all around. Here and there a scattering of dandelion seeds on the wind.

Rose is there, arms reaching out on each side of her body, as if to embrace all that she can see.

Don't rush. She's there, all's well.

She's seen me. She's recognized me.

She has turned back to the sea. From on top of this tall cliff the view is breathtaking. She's humming a tune. I strain to hear it against the wind.

Now, up on the tall cliff, I'm Rose at all ages and in every shape and form, a multiple Rose, an archipelago of shifting memories.

Here, I'm my mother.

I'm my mother at twenty-one, at the cliff edge, a gust of salt air on my face. My hair is hers, flying about my head, whisked across my forehead before it's caught by another gust. She was grey already, and she had a few sparse strands of white. She was young to be turning grey, to have that sprinkling of white hair. It's in the family. My hair, which went white long ago, is hers, swept by the salt air, for I'm my mother at twenty-one, my mother at the edge of the high cliff.

On my mother's skin I can feel the buffeting wind, the lash of the tall, salt grass, and the blazing sunlight.

On my mother's skin I can feel the dandelion seeds that barely tickle, and then only when we see them brush our calves, our knees, our thighs, here, our arms, even, when the island wind mingles its tremor with the wind off the sea.

On my new motherly skin I feel the hem of the flowered dress she wore that day, and the silky petticoat that made each step a caress. Wantonly, they flap around me.

I can feel the salt-cotton from the open sea on the skin of my vanished mother, weaving me a cocoon. That means nothing, there's no such thing as salt-cotton. But I feel it come clinging to my body, to my mother's body.

I can't smell her perfume, my mother's scent, on my mother's fugitive skin. As though it was invariably lost amid odours from the past. Lavender soap. Bread dough and yeast. And the fragrant cedar of the old wardrobe, and all the spices it couldn't hold. Eau de cologne, Papa's, the fragrance he sprinkled on his face, morning and evening, shaken from the white bottle into his callused hands and then carried to his sometimes unshaven cheeks, just to smell good, just for Mama to want to come to him, so that she would tell him he smelled good, so that she would maybe feel like kissing him.

He often told me about that.

About the joy it meant for him. When she raised her eyes from the soft outline of the coast to meet with his. When he could seduce the woman who filled the volume of his days. When she was in a mood to smile. When her body danced more than usual, making her hems fly beside the kitchen table. When she hummed. When she whistled too. When she let him approach her from behind. To lay one hand on her hip, the other on her belly. To brush her nape with his lips, and tickle her with his moustache. Then she'd close her eyes and continue humming or whistling. And she'd turn her head, eyes closed, offering her mouth, eyes closed, for him to kiss, freely, at last.

Till she opened her eyes, and her mood changed.

He often told me about that. When his evening drunkenness was a perch held out to me, a perch I'd take to climb on his knees. With my head resting on his lean, hairy chest, my ear thrust into the opening of his unbuttoned shirt, listening to the unfathomable source of his voice.

He often told me about it, before his eyes streamed drunken tears, and then he'd drink some more, to dry his tear ducts. And when finally he'd downed enough rotgut, he'd push the heavy table against the counter and start dancing in the kitchen, then bawl the drinking songs or shanties he'd learned from Gérard on the Brandy Pot, when he was the assistant keeper.

> *dondaine laridaine*
> *matapate talimatou*
> *matantalou malimatou*
> *matapate alimatou*
> *matantalo elaridé*

And then it was a party, and I'd dance with him, drunk as well, drunk on fatigue and delight, and we were no longer alone, with the leaping shadows of our bodies around us, thrown onto the wall by the glow of the fire. The shadow of my body flying at the end of his strangely long arms.

> *dondaine laridaine*
> *matapate talimatou*
> *matantalou malimatou*
> *matapate alimatou*
> *matantalo elaridé*

And I'd dance with him, sing with him, till we went out on the veranda, breathless and sweating, to collapse into a landscape swept by blue moonlight. We'd remain like that, me in his arms, he in his thoughts, staring at the stars or losing ourselves in the fog, or gazing at the lights sparkling on the coast, until he ordered me to bed.

Daughter, it's time. Go to bed.

And I'd go up, as weightless as before in his arms. Still flying in my mind and on the narrow staircase leading to my room.

People don't know what they say. On the island, nothing is ever really cut off. There's too much horizon around, and too much carrying wind.

My mother knew that. In spite of everything. My mother the bird knew that.

I'm my mother at twenty-one. With my arms beating the air like the wild branches of a larch tree. Now I'm a cross on the headland, a cross of flesh at the very top, making the island into a cathedral like the ones that crane their necks upwards in cities, but without all the other buildings around to smother it.

From here I overlook the eastern point of the island, the river where its horizon is vastest, my missing mother's body, and all the tears that have washed it, before and after its plunge to the river water.

I am my mother amid the green fragrance of the hazel bushes, with the wind ruffling my hair into my face and eyes; I'm here, disoriented, like when she lost her footing, when a stone rolled, when the wind pushed her, or perhaps it was despair; I am she, beating the air with her arms just before the fall, gazing down into the water below, with her hair in her eyes, the wind in her hair, her dress in the breeze, the sea in the folds of her dress. I am she, before her body is grazed and broken on the stones piled at the base of the steep cliff, rocked by the bloody sea water. I am she before her body was lost for hours. Lost. For hours.

And then, for a moment, I'm just myself, an old woman kneeling among the wildflowers fed by the open sea and the salt grasses, weeping though I have seen nothing, not the body below, nor the blood, down on my knees, crying out among the wildflowers, dying in my turn.

And for this moment I become myself again, a little girl, watching Papa in tears as he digs a grave with his bare hands. Grazing his hands on the rock. Loosening the rock of his anger. The anger of a man always alone, since forever.

I am me, the child, that Papa takes in his arms before the little pile of earth heaped on Mama's body carried to the clifftop. Me, the little girl, gazing at a makeshift cross of hemlock boards scorched by the sun and tied with a sailor's knot. A cross with no epitaph.

I am my mother in reverse, standing at the edge of the cliff, but this time I won't jump. I won't join the broth swirling on the stones below. I'll remain here, resplendent.

I begin to weep again in the wind. I am my mother, living and breathing again.

The thing I'm looking at isn't down below.

The thing I'm looking at is farther off. A lot farther. It's the coast, with its music. It's an unrecognizable village, lost in its memories, a village that tells a lying story of itself, one like me. One just like me.

What I'm looking at is also somewhere else. It's a liar of a window that can see everything, show everything, and show it badly: an alley boxed in between the corrugated-iron sheds, the puddles in every corner, like tear-filled eyes, a child passing with two lobes to his right ear, and a neighbour worried about her washing that hasn't dried before the sun is snuffed out between a few clouds that threaten rain, and white sheets flapping on the line.

What I'm looking at is here too. It's my eyes dried by the breeze, and a man I'm not sure I recognize, as happens to me sometimes. And it's a young black woman at the foot of the cliff, raising her lovely head in my direction. Her smile, so eloquent.

Everything's fine. Everything will be fine.

NOTES ON THE TRANSLATION

In *The Keeper's Daughter*, names – and changes of name, for the uncertainty of identity is a theme of the novel – are important. In real life, names are labels that serve to identify people, places, and things; in fiction, however, names are chosen by the author, and sometimes they carry a second meaning corresponding to a trait of the fictional character or place. However, it is rarely appropriate, or even possible, to translate names, so that in such cases something is inevitably "lost in translation."

The Quebec village on which the story of Rose Brouillard centres was originally called Sainte-Marie, but it has been renamed Sainte-Marée-de-l'Incantation. "Marie," the French name for the Virgin Mary, is replaced by *marée* ("tide"). The name would almost certainly remind a Québécois reader of Marie de l'Incarnation, a Ursuline nun and missionary to Aboriginal peoples in seventeenth-century New France, whose name has been given to many streets and buildings, though not to any real Quebec village. In the novel, the new name is bestowed by Plumules Nord, the company that has transformed the village into a tourist attraction and invented the bogus ritual of the "incantation." Although plumule signifies "down feather," the verb *plumer* ("to pluck") also means "to cheat," suggesting there is something not quite above board about the firm's activities. A motel on the way to Sainte-Marée is called "Motel Pèlerins" – perhaps encouraging tourists to think of themselves as pilgrims (*pèlerins*) and of Sainte-Marée as a genuine holy site – which of course it is not.

Where the characters are concerned, Rose Brouillard's last name is particularly apt for someone often lost in the fog of her dementia, for *brouillard* means "fog." A major portion of the story is told through the eyes and camera lens of "Dorothée," a young woman of Haitian origin, whose real name we never learn. In Rose's mind she has become confused with the women of colour who appear in the poetry of Charles Baudelaire: one, whom the poet knew on the island of Réunion, during a voyage to the Indian Ocean (hence "the African girl"), is evoked in a poem called "La Belle Dorothée"; another was Baudelaire's mistress, Jeanne Duval, whom the poet compares to a sensuous cat: Rose also refers to "Dorothée" as "Baudelaire's cat." Monsieur Vignault's three female cousins are named Flore (the French name for the Roman goddess of flowers), Marguerite ("Daisy"), and Jacinthe ("Hyacinth"), which explains the whimsical reference to them as "the three flowers" and a "floral chorus."

Some brief explanations of other aspects of Francophone culture evoked in the novel may be useful.

"Marianne" (page 35) is a personification of the French revolutionary ideal of liberty, often identified with the figure in the famous painting by Delacroix, *Liberty Leading the People*. *The Origin of the World* is a painting by Gustave Courbet which depicts the lower abdomen and genitals of a reclining female nude. *A Country without Hats* (page 47) is a novel by Dany Laferrière (born 1953), a Quebec writer of Haitian origin, while Jacques Roumain's *Gouverneurs de la rosée* (1944) is a classic of Haitian literature. Some traditional Quebec and French dishes with no equivalents in Anglophone cuisine are mentioned (page 54): *cipaille* (a Québécois multi-layered pie generally made with a variety of meats, sometimes including game); *bouilli* (a stew of beef, pork, cabbage, potatoes, carrots, and so on); and *ratatouille* (a stew of eggplant, zucchini, and tomatoes). Professor Calculus (page 77) is a character in the *Tintin* comic books. Marc Aurèle Fortin (page 85) was a Quebec painter (1888–1970) whose work is somewhat reminiscent of the Group of Seven. André Mathieu (page 93) was a Quebec pianist and composer (1929–1968): a child prodigy, he gave his first public recital in a Montreal hotel a few days after his sixth birthday. Two of Baudelaire's poems are quoted: four lines (in translation) of "Une charogne," which describes the rotting corpse of an animal (page 81), and a line from "Invitation au voyage": *luxe, calme, et volupté* – "luxury, calm, and sensual pleasure" (page 122). Lines from two traditional French folksongs have been translated: "La belle Françoise" (page 75), and "À la claire fontaine" (page 110). The reference to a song about swallows (page 74) probably refers to another folksong, "Ah toi, belle hirondelle," in which a swallow carries a message from a young woman to her absent lover.

We hope that, thanks to this information, for readers of *The Keeper's Daughter* a little less will be lost in the translation.

ABOUT THE TRANSLATOR

W. Donald Wilson was born in County Fermanagh, Northern Ireland, and took a degree in modern languages (French and German) at Trinity College, Dublin, and after a graduate year in Paris, returned to Trinity College, where he also completed a Ph.D. in modern French literature. He taught at the University of the West Indies, in Jamaica, and at the University of Liverpool before coming to Canada in 1970 to the University of Waterloo, where he was also chair of the department of French studies for several years. He took early retirement in 1996, and since then has been devoting some of his time to literary translation, both fiction and non-fiction. In 2011 and 2013 two of Wilson's translations were long-listed for the Best Translated Book Award in the United States, and in 2013 he was a finalist for the French-American Foundation translation prize. His translation of Jacques Chessex's novel *Un juif pour l'exemple* won an award from the Looren Foundation (Switzerland).

ABOUT THE AUTHOR

Jean-François Caron was born in La Pocatière, Quebec, in 1978. In 2005, after several rewarding years as a teacher of French, he became editor-in-chief of *Voir Saguenay/Alma*, where he spent five years as cultural correspondent and columnist. He then worked as a freelance writer, contributing regularly to other Quebec periodicals, including *Lettres québécoises*, *Vie des arts*, and *Le Sabord*. He has also written several artist's books and exhibition catalogues, some of which have been published by Sagamie – Éditions d'art. In 2010 he assumed responsibility for communications and audience development for Théatre La Rubrique, in Jonquière. Editor-in chief of *L'Unique*, the journal of the Quebec Union of Writers, he also belongs to the editorial board of *Lettres québécoises*, for which he writes a regular feature.

The author of two books of poetry and a first novel, *Nos échoueries* (La Peuplade, 2010), Caron has been awarded several literary prizes for both fiction and poetry. In 2008 he received a master's degree in literary studies and creation from the Université du Québec in Chicoutimi. At present he lives and works in the relative isolation of Sainte-Béatrix, in the Lanaudière region of Quebec, where he devotes himself to writing.